Page 2

The

PHOENIX

Experiment

AARON RYAN

Author of the bestselling post-apocalyptic alien invasion saga *Dissonance*, the award-winning Christian dystopian fiction saga *The End,* the *Talisman* series, the sci-fi thrillers *Forecast* and *The Slide*, *God is Not Santa, The Christian Kids Values, Identity & Affirmation Picture Book Series* and many more.

Published in 2025, Edition 1.

eBook ISBN # 9781965372418 · Paperback ISBN # 9781965372425
Hardcover ISBN # 9781965372432

Edited by CM LLC. Published independently.

Cover art by Aaron Ryan & CM LLC. Phoenix bird licensed for unlimited reproduction / print runs through iStock on License #490651863

This is a work of fiction. Any similarities to persons living or dead, or actual events is purely coincidental.

For Sweeps, Bren & AJ:
my true loves.

Thank you for helping me to rise from the ashes.

Chapters

"If only one could have two lives… one in which to make one's mistakes… the second in which to profit by them."

D.H. Lawrence

Note on AI

We live in an age of AI. Every day, more and more services spring up promising revolutionary and innovative results using artificial intelligence. The authoring industry is not immune to this.

I want every one of my readers to know that not once did I employ, nor will I *ever* employ, the use of AI to sculpt any part of any of my stories. Those who know me know that I am staunchly and adamantly opposed to such cheats.

I'm very proud to be a verified human. The ability to create is a gift that I was endowed by my Creator, and I will never forfeit that nor set it aside to propagate something synthetic and imitative.

Everything you've read by me in this novel, and in my other works, is 100% entirely created by me, the genuine article. I'm a verified human, and always will be.

To my fellow authors, I urge you to preserve the sacred gift of human creation and never stoop to such lows. Always cherish this gift you've been given. If you encounter writer's block, take a break. Don't cop out. Don't take the road more traveled by. Don't cheat. Toe the line for all of us, and keep creation – *true* unadulterated creation – alive.

Long live humanity.

Also, if you're an author – or even a budding one – I'd love to personally extend an invite to you to join me in two unique groups on Facebook: the "Authors &

Writers ONLY" group of which I am the admin, and my own personal group, the "Author Aaron Ryan Group." The first group is one where you can connect with thousands of other authors across the globe, ask questions, learn and grow as a writer, and network. Grapes grow best in bunches, after all.

And the second is my own personal group. I find much higher engagement in my *group* than with my Facebook *page*. I also welcome other authors to enter there for free giveaways, news, and also to learn why I self-publish, what benefits there are in being a writer-entrepreneur, and more. As a fellow author, I'm always there to help you in any way I can.

God bless you as you use the gift of creation to write your stories. May they, and you, be utterly successful.

Sincerely,

Aaron Ryan,
Verified Human

Note on Faith

I am a Christian author. What does that mean exactly?
It means I worship Jesus, and I serve my God in
Heaven. That implies certain standards should be
upheld, and that my life should be lived in certain
ways, with certain morals, by certain convictions, and
with a sense of honoring God in all I do and in all I
write. I seek to tell **true** and inspiring stories.

One thing I've always strived for is verisimilitude.
I've wanted my books to be on par with what we read

out there in the world: to be adventurous escapism, to provide a gritty sense of reality, and to provide a real glimpse into the ebbs and flows of the struggles that humanity faces. That means that life isn't always glimpsed through rose-colored stained-glass windows. It means that with the good comes the gory. With the sheer valor comes the shock value. With the awe comes the awful. Does that then mean that I will ever drop an F-Bomb or take my Lord's name in vain in my works? **Never**. But does it mean that I will bury my head in the sand and pretend that we humans down here don't talk a certain way, walk a certain way, act a certain way? **Never**.

I want my works to reflect the real, genuine authentic struggles that humans face, and as such I want the real, genuine, authentic reactions that come with being human. If an alien is going to eat you, you might not say "Oh, shucks." You might say something, hmm, *a bit more colorful.* But I want my readers to know that I've always struggled with this, and do not mean to offend anyone with material some might find objectionable. I'm a Christian, but I'm also an artist, and artists seek to stretch themselves and strive for truth and reality in their works. That does **not** mean that I need to go overboard and pepper you with revolting material or words that Christians have no business engaging or indulging in. As such, I want all of my faith-based readers to know that I am highly conscious of what I put out there into the world, and am constantly checking it against my spirit before I do so.

Nothing you'll read in my novels is much different from what we experience on this ball in space, and I trust you'll see that I've walked a fine line here, and I ask for your forgiveness if I've offended you in any way. I pray this work of mine provides you with an awesome and incredible odyssey of escapism and adventure. I pray you are moved at times by the Holy Spirit as you read. I pray that you understand God better, and that you know that God knows my heart, and I tried my best to tell a **real** story, understanding that we're all down here, **all** of us, just trying to do our very best in creating what we feel led to create.

I thank you **so** much for reading my novel.

In Jesus' Name,

Aaron Ryan

PART ONE:
Out of the Frying Pan

1: The Origin

In the vast blackness of space, one knows only peace.

I lie here in The Origin, this overlarge and sleek G-class science vessel: a star-freighter, really, but not big enough to call a floating city. It has more than enough space to allow me to wander, but not enough for me to get *really* lost.

For a 14-year-old boy like me, however, getting lost is always part of the fun. Anther is the same way.

As I dimly come to consciousness, I'm cognizant once more of the quiet beeps of life-sustaining devices all around me, and the sensors attached to my skin monitoring heart rate and rhythm, blood pressure, pulse oximetry, body temperature, respiratory rate, glucose levels, movement, brain activity, and the like.

The IV in my arm dispenses that wonderful serum, and it's always a relatively rude awakening coming out of cryo-sleep from it. Sleep-cycles are necessary to keep us alive out here: we cherish them and guard them ferociously. When they're over for the night, it's an inescapable disappointment. Not because we don't get to sleep anymore, though. That's not the reason. It's because we don't get to dream the dreams we want.

Without the specific dreams, all you have left is the fading memories.

I feel my eyes dilate as they acclimate to the harsh light. The forced REM cycles brought on by the serum are always welcome, because the calm is *soooo* good, but it's equally *soooo* hard being ripped out of it. Always seems to happen right before the really good parts too, *dang it.*

I blink stupidly in the light, looking around slowly, dimly taking in my surroundings once more: sterile white and antiseptic as I float here in this translucent jelly. It stinks every single time I get out of here and wash off: a mashup of something that smells like a crude mixture of ketchup and detergent. I'm familiar with detergent because we wash our uniforms with it. But I barely remember the taste of ketchup, although I do remember the horrid smell. There was a younger orphan on The Origin once who, before he came to us, ate nothing *but* ketchup. He would order a hot dog, smother it in ketchup, and literally lick all the ketchup off and leave the dog. I throw up in my mouth a little just thinking about it. He was ultimately successful, and got to go back. I can't wait to wash off the scent and get back to business as usual.

And I can't wait to go back, too.

The Phoenix Experiments. You would think for a teenager they would be an irritating and eye-rolling obligation, but I'm better than that. I enjoy them. I should: after all, it's an opportunity for them to get better acquainted with Jax Hutson, the star of the show.

Me.

There are all kinds of posts you can sign up for when you're conscripted at age 8. All kinds of choices exist to tickle your fancy. Some are more demanding than others. Most align with your personality profile and life experiences at that age. For me, The Origin was a no-brainer.

I didn't sign up for this post because I wanted to; I signed up because I *had* to.

Because, if there's even the slightest chance that they can come back, I owe it to them, no matter the length of time it takes.

I miss them.

I miss them with all my heart.

The shower feels wonderfully refreshing as always. This is the best part of my day, feeling those warm rivulets coursing over me and sending tingles down my body. I feel most alive during these brief, private times. Moreover, I feel *clean*: the disgusting ketchup goo is washed off of me and then collected in the reservoir beneath my feet for analysis by The Origin. I take a deep breath and close my eyes, enjoying it while I can, before the 0900 chow call.

I finish up and towel off in the Hygiene Block, which we call the HB for short. There are a few others in here with me.

There's Garris: he's a big 15-year-old oaf who adds two and two together and somehow gets chicken. I don't understand how his Neanderthal mind works, nor how he got on this ship. Also, I think he still pees in his sleep.

Then there's Ranshay: a diminutive and quiet 12-year-old kid who I know is a brainiac because Anther and I stole a look at his test scores, but you'd never know it because he doesn't speak a lick of English. Which begs the question: how does he even understand what he's being taught in order to score so highly? I shake my head in disbelief as I glance at him.

Next, there's Martos: a spunky 16-year-old who likes to be the life of the party but who tires quickly: an extrovert who abruptly runs out of steam before his ship ever reaches the dock.

And finally, I spot Venthix. He's alright. I've had a few conversations with him; he seems like a good guy. He's 15.

Not everyone is here. Anther Secto is my best friend, but he's nowhere to be found this morning.

All of us are on this ship for one simple reason, and we all know what it is.

Sadly, there are no girls on The Origin. I hate that. They're not allowed here, in order to, as they say, 'keep us focused.' Whatever. We know why we're here, and that's plenty focus enough. A double-Y chromosome environment is so static and boring; way too many farts and not enough perfume to combat them. To my knowledge there haven't *ever* been females on The Origin… they're all over on The Zephyr on the other side of Earth's orbit.

There are also so very few of us onboard The Origin. Just four adults, a synthetic, a rumored engineer whom no one ever sees, and the eight of us boys. For a ship this size, you would think there would be more staff, engineers, technicians, or the like, to assume maintenance duties, but it's highly unnecessary. The Origin is, for all intents and purposes, self-sustaining. Rumors persist that the engineer is an elderly female, as odd as that sounds. I have never seen her, so I can't say.

The Origin – and The Zephyr, for that matter – is a sentient ship that literally feels like a living presence in every single corridor, quarters or compartment this ship presents. Violin and flute concerto music plays everywhere, incessantly. Sitars sometimes join in. Whoever wrote the schematics for this place was intent on a tranquil environment with soothing vibes permeating the whole of the ship, always. I've been here for five years and there are areas that are still new and interesting. AI is prevalent throughout, as creepy as that is. But Phiria sounds human, and she knows what's going on with The Origin at all times. She's also surprisingly conversational, and she remembers.

AI is unavoidable anymore. I mean, it's 2471, for goodness' sake. By now, AI is everywhere *anyway*, and all the naysayers have finally been won over. At least, I *think* they have.

Historical records assert that there was a prolonged flirtation with – and profound *resistance* to – AI, in the early years of the 21st century. Especially by creators who felt they were being replaced by automation. Can't say I blame them. I wouldn't want to be replaced, either. But that's the world we live in anymore, right? Upgrades, synthetics, and replacements. The Origin teems with all kinds of life, real and fake, which makes sense, given its name.

The only thing you can't really replace is a human soul. At least, not yet.

And that's precisely why I'm here.

I don't know when I first started hearing them. It was a few years ago, but whether they started coming in my subconscious, in my sleep, or in my waking life, I still have no idea. It's a dim, chanting voice: breathy and calm, alluring and mysterious, at times brimming with pathos, and always with a note of urgency and clarity. I have given up questioning why I hear the voice, and why it speaks to me in poetry and prose, because I find it utterly captivating.

These mental permeations come fairly often; a voice whispering to me from beyond. I don't know if it's a byproduct of The Phoenix Experiment or not, or if I'm the only one who hears the calm chanting. I'm content not to find out, however, as it isn't exactly irritating. It's just a constant reminder of where we are, and it comes at unawares and odd times.

And here it comes yet again.

> *In the vast expanse of time*
> *Suffering and discontent combine*
> *Until the quell,*
> *no voice shall tell*
> *Serene, sweet resolution's clime*
>
> *So thus, they wander, aimless, hoping*

> *Trying, dreaming, striving, hoping*
> *Keeping on*
> *whilst sleeping long*
> *Phoenix rising, talons groping*

My mind snaps back from the reverie.

I know exactly where I am. It's the same every day, but you get used to it. The walls are white, the floors are white, the ceiling is white, and the air I breathe is practically white as well, sanitized and antiseptic, optimized and perfected for life in space. It 'tastes' lighter than the air I would breathe down on Earth, especially in the big cities where the air is so thick you can chew it. But I don't really remember the air down there anyway. Eventually, you get used to it up here, and this air is all you know.

Chow time is another matter. It's something I have never really gotten used to, and I'm not looking forward to it today, either. They feed us *BioPrime*: a revolting and boring goo composed of amino acids, proteins and everything a growing body needs, sure, but it looks like the same stuff we float in, and I swear it smells like it, too.

What is it with ketchupy stuff everywhere, anyway? I think to myself as I head that way. It's been perfected, and I'm sure it has everything a body needs, but it's monotonous, dull, and same ol' same ol.' The lack of variety is irritating. At least it comes in more than a few fruit flavors, so I suppose I should be grateful. But I'm not.

I suppose I should *also* be grateful since many are starving down there on Earth. But, just *once*, I'd love to sink my teeth into that little thing called 'steak' that I've heard so much about. Never had one. I don't suppose I ever will. The Origin isn't about quick results… or even guaranteed ones. We're all here 'til we age out at 18. Anyway, I'm also told steak isn't even a breakfast food, not that that matters.

I look forward to hanging with Anther at breakfast. He's my best friend, and he's my age. I didn't request that; it just worked out that way and drew us together. No complaints from me. He's about my height, but I'm a blonde and he's a brunette, I'm skinny and he's bulky, I'm spry and he's a klutz. It has also been observed that I'm articulate and a chutzpah-laden spitfire; Anther, however, has been playfully labeled a 'lovable meathead.'

He seems oblivious to the fact that I'm the one who came up with that label. I decide never to tell him.

I received the highest score on the AG. The Aptitude Gauntlet isn't what people make it out to be. I think back to it now, and can't remember any of the specific questions, other than a general memory that they dealt with computation and syntax, reasoning and vocabulary. I also completed it before any of my peers did. The fact that they make all of us go through it at the tender age of 6 seems barbaric; cruel and unusual punishment for those still amassing knowledge and life training. But *que sera, sera*: they need to know that our aptitude is greater than a box of hair before they bring us onboard The Origin. Can't have all those kids blowing a gasket in The Phoenix Experiments. Which, again, stupefies me that someone like Garris is here.

Anther's an orphan as well, like all of us are, so we share that trauma, not that we asked for it. We'd much prefer to have our parents back. But fate, it seems, is what decided to bring us together in trauma, and trauma makes for a good binding agent for hurting souls like ours.

There he is. Anther's already gotten his 'breakfast,' and is sitting down at a table close to the chow hall entrance. He lifts his hand and hails me. "Sup," he says with a warm smile and a slouch. I greet him back with similar jocularity, and play slug him in the shoulder. "Ow," he grunts, but he's beefy enough to absorb the hit. I didn't use my full force anyway. If I had, Anther would surely be dead.

I motion over to the chow line and he nods, assured that I'll be back in a minute for a hearty mutual partaking of our revolting health slop. *BioPrime.* Ick.

In a few more moments I receive a full dosage serving from the dispenser. This time I opt for strawberry flavor. I wish it was real strawberries and not some crude *caricature* of strawberries.

I plop down next to Anther. He smells like ketchup and detergent, so I assume he hasn't showered. *So that's where he was this morning,* I think to myself. *Not* showering. I detect a faint whiff of body odor as well, but shake it off. This is not the first time.

"How was your sleep?" I ask, nonchalantly, before downing a spoonful. I practically hold my nose as I do so.

"Fine," he shrugs, but I see that he's actually downplaying it. He stifles a chortle.

"Yeah, *right*," I tease.

Anther can't suppress his enthusiasm. It was there when he greeted me entering the cafeteria. It's obvious to me that *she* made another appearance, and now he tries to get me to pry it out of him. Anther explodes with joy and turns to me. "Haha! You can tell, can't you? It was *awesome,* dude."

"Okay, okay, *out* with it, man. Did she tell you her name yet or not?"

A huge grin spreads across his face. "You know me too well, bro. *No!* I mean, *yes,* she was there, but no, she didn't tell me her name yet. Man, I wish she was here on The Origin with us. That girl is *hot*. No joke. I mean, like otherworldly hot. Too bad she's just a dream." He chuckles, and I echo it. Desperate fool. I'm not sure which I'm laughing at more: his obsession or his desperation.

But… I actually *do* wish I could meet her.

I haven't met anyone that tantalizing yet in my own sleep cycles *or* in The Phoenix Experiments. Anther could be lying, of course, but that would be atypical for him. All of us boys want a hot girl in our dreams. Maybe he's just the first to get lucky.

"*Otherworldly* hot, huh? I bet she has an otherworldly cool name then, as well. Like *Stellanova*, or, or…," -here I try my hand at a creative name after a star system- "*Aurelia Centauri* or something like that."

Anther chuckles again. "Yeah! I bet. I'll find out, eventually, I'm sure."

"What was she wearing this time?" I prod.

"Nothing," he jests almost immediately, and I seize the opportunity to elbow him jealously.

"Shut up!"

Anther is just brimming with giggles this morning. "Kidding. I wish."

"Yeah, you wish, indeed."

Anther looks at me comically.

"Okay, okay, I wish too," I laugh sheepishly.

Part of me wonders if that part of Anther's story is actually true, and he's just being coy. But whatever. I move on, a little wrecked inside that I haven't had my own serum-induced hot girl dream yet. The serum they give us is potent, but, as with anything, *results may vary*. Maybe he's just hornier than I am. I privately resolve to work on that, but deep inside I suspect The Origin staff is holding out on me.

For the time being, however, I still want my parents back more than I want a girl.

It's true. And I secretly hope that Anther understands that as much as I need him to. But who am I kidding? I know he does. Pop his parents or his siblings into that dream in place of that girl? He'd be a blubbering wreck, just like we all would.

Chow time is done, so I brush my teeth and then get ready to report to Stygius Cryptus. The science officer is no one to be trifled with, and I do *not* want to be late. He does his job with mathematical precision and all the warmth of a kitchen knife. His breath reeks of sardines and foods that I frequently find myself overly curious about, wondering a) how he got ahold of them, and b) why, to date, we're still limited to protein goo for the meals that *we* get. *Maybe they're not real sardines,* I think to myself.

Leaving those thoughts aside, I make my way to Quadrant C, Subfloor 3A, Room 319. It's close to our dorms. The Phoenix Experiments call, but a yearning stirs within me to run and explore the bowels of The Origin once more. I know it's forbidden, however, and would be counterproductive.

The last time Anther and I did so, Helmsman Fulsar Oculus scolded us for a pretty half-hour, then confined us to quarters with no rec allowance for three days. Recreation passes the time here so well, and is *never* to be missed. That chastisement, though brief, thoroughly sucked. Nonetheless, it didn't stop Anther. He's been in and out of the vent shafts more times than I can count, and it's like he knows this ship like the back of his hand now.

Oculus is a fat and aging man, balding. There's nothing attractive about him. His Australian accent is thick and roguish, as if he's got a perpetual repository of gravel midway down his throat. He constantly reeks of something that might be equated to alcohol, but no one can blame him. He's been the steward of this ship longer than The Phoenix Experiment has even been in operation.

First Officer Argin Mirabay is his mirror opposite: composed, stoic, rigid, quiet, and half Oculus' age. He's also intimidating, but not in the same way as our synthetic.

Room 319. I've arrived. I round the corner. There's Cryptus, sitting calm and collected, with a stare that reflects nothing. I glance silently past him into the lab, with the chairs, the chambers, the electrodes, the connections, and more gadgetry than I can pretend to understand. Cryptus knows what it all does, however. All I know is that I get to go back to sleep in there, and when I do, this time I get to dream dreams that are *mine*. There's no serum; there's no manipulation other than a psychological profiling beforehand that allows me to reconnect with sweet memories of my parents. And then the white noise kicks in and the deep throbbing that puts us in a subconscious state as we're thrust into the center of the ring. It's irresistible. You don't fight it. It's pointless to. Besides, we all want to get back in there.

Cryptus likes to meditate. Like, a lot. I can't figure out what he's meditating on, specifically, nor do

I understand why he cherishes the activity so much. I already have peace, as much as can be expected. But, with a name like *Stygius Cryptus*, maybe one could expect to be slightly more troubled than your average synthetic. Or, maybe it's a power-saving thing and he needs to conserve battery or something.

I silently wait at the entrance to the android's office, unwilling to disturb him. His office is impeccable, and he guards it like a gentle Cerberus. Everything is in its place, and he would know swiftly if you rotated a pen by a single degree. When we were younger, Anther and I used to play-act like I was Cryptus and he was Oculus. He would fiddle with something in our boys' quarters, and I would accusingly tell him what it was, remonstrating him with a constrained, android wrath.

I watch him, silently standing there and trying to match his breathing with my own. I close my eyes and try to purge the noise as I demonstrate my own prowess at meditation. His breathy voice stabs through my head with an alarming suddenness that makes me jump.

"Welcome, Jax," he greets me, eventually, and I lurch from the quiet, surprise salutation punctuating my own attempt at meditation. It is almost as if he was just waiting for me to drift into serenity so that he could call my name and jolt me back to awareness. Something in me tells me that was exactly his plan.

"I didn't move your pen!" I blurt out, jarred with eyes wide. I correct myself and shuffle. "Uh, I mean, he-hello, Cryptus," I stammer uneasily, looking up and finding him coldly surveying me.

"Fascinating," he mutters, his eyes narrowing. "I am, in fact, missing a pen. I shall assume, for now, that you have stolen it. Should you discover the ability to magically produce one, Jax," he pauses for effect, emphasizing my name, "I shall be grateful. I prefer blue ink, as you may recall." His eyes narrow.

That thick British brogue is so intriguing, and yet so dully patronizing. I'm well aware that Cryptus' programming equips him to take on any accent at any time, and he could have just lectured me as an elderly Caribbean woman if that was his wish. But he chooses British, ostensibly because he can condescend to all of us underlings. It also matches his expressionless and intimidating visage perfectly.

"Thanks, I, uh, do recall that," I say, uneasily.

Blue ink. The accusation isn't lost on me. Anther and I had once spied on him in here while he conducted a Phoenix experiment on Ranshay, and, unbeknownst to both of us, Anther's pen leaked right out of his pocket and right through the vent we were spying through. Cryptus has good eyes *and* good ears, and he could hear that blue ink spilling right through the grate. He whirled to face us. We shrieked and took off. He caught us at the vent aperture and confronted us. I still tremble thinking back to that.

"Shall we begin?" he asks me, and his expression instantly morphs into a put-on smile. Cryptus bounds up without waiting for my answer.

"This way," he directs, though I know the way and have been in the chamber countless times already.

"Yes," I mumble. I find myself intimidated around Cryptus, though I know I shouldn't still be so daunted by him. I'm never intimidated around anyone else except Oculus. But Cryptus has this unnerving quality to him, being a synthetic: so pompous, supercilious and condescending. I don't ever feel like I'm 14; I always feel like I'm 4… *and in trouble.*

He holds the door open for me, and I walk nervously past him. "Any containment issues last night?" he inquires in a disinterested monotone.

I shake my head. "None."

As protocol, we're supposed to report any containment anomalies to Cryptus immediately upon awakening, filing a report in the stasis log next to our pod. I tell him that I haven't had any.

This, of course, is a lie, but I don't tell Cryptus that. The truth of the matter is that my parents have been in practically every single dream I've ever had since they died that hot August day five years ago, and this is the force within me that keeps me going, I know that. To surrender that? To pretend like they're not there? It would be like allowing them to die all over again, and that's a concession I'm not prepared to make. Cryptus doesn't have to know. What he doesn't know won't short out his circuits.

The android surveys me uncomfortably and lengthily, staring into my eyes as if equipped with a visual polygraph. I feel like I'm about to squirm. But thankfully, I've perfected my blank slate expression to a fault, and we reach an impasse.

The synthetic relents with a mild *hmmm*, and allows me to pass. I continue on into the chamber and mount up in the left seat, the first of three in there. I know the reason there are three. So does Cryptus. So does every single orphan onboard The Origin. The third chair is different from the other two, and it is encased in a chamber with a lot of gadgets and wiring.

Cryptus says nothing to me as he mechanically goes about his duty, strapping me in and wiring me up for The Phoenix Experiment. This is, after all, what he was made for; it's his driving purpose here, and it is, after all, the whole reason I'm here.

The Phoenix Experiments were made as a way to connect with what was lost; to restore purpose and affirmation, contentment and closure for those bereaved. The 'phoenix' label was meant as a symbol of rebirth for those entering the experiments, so that they could receive their closure, breathe the free air again, and start over, brand new. A novel concept, to be sure.

I don't remember offhand who conceived of it, but I'm glad they did. Somebody named Joseph or Giuseppe or Jonas or something, back in 2234. Back then, I think it was called 'Cairon,' in honor of the Greek mythological ferryman whose job it was to guide souls across the river Styx. The intent, both then and now, is to try to connect the bereaved with the passed in a serene setting, allowing us to enter a state of dreamlike calm and visit 'the other side.' To, essentially, *ferry* us over to our loved ones, and then return us back to the real world. We're in a state of suspended animation while we sojourn there. It's amazing, every single time, but would be even more so if I could actually find my parents.

Call it, 'counseling in catatonia,' if you will. The body is supposedly more able to make peace with a situation in a dreamlike state. Situations become idealized and resolutions are more dramatic and memorable, ultimately translating into waking life. For a planet still recovering from unimaginable loss and misfortune, The Phoenix Experiments promote health in tangible ways, creating young citizens who will be stronger for their eventual return to Earth.

I know full well the reason why they need us to be stronger. Earth needs more Speakers. The monsters are still out there, and they've taken too many of us. Trauma and bereavement can limit us; they leave us aching. Being freed of that trauma harnesses our focus. Banshees feed on yearning, and those who are bereaved… well, *yearn*. It's that simple. Take away the yearning, and banshees can't zero us.

So, naturally, if we find a way to perfect speaking to the dead, we'll be invaluable assets back on Earth. Speakers are always in high demand. Mature, non-conflicted Speakers can pacify the dead *and* the banshees. My purpose here doesn't dampen my desire to reconnect with my parents in the here and now; for the moment, I care far more about that.

Cryptus is the perfect moderator for these experiments: he's cold and unfeeling, and assigns neither angst nor jubilation to any of his subjects' reactions. He monitors us plainly, ambivalently, medically, noting sweat secretion and heartbeat arrhythmia indicating excitement due to emotional reconnection, and then calmly observing a return to normal heart rate and body temperature, which indicates the work is done. Rumor has it he can actually enter with us if he wanted to, in some sort of dream link, but I've never seen it done.

Then he pulls us out, back into the real world, where our parents cannot come and no longer exist once more, except in memory. The more progress we make separating from the yearning, the stronger we'll be in the end.

The only sad part about all of this is, to date, I've never once found my parents in any of my experiments. In the Phoenix Experiments, you're still awake, focused, and present. Things can happen within your control.

In the Phoenix Experiments, you can actually bring them back.

I just can't seem to find them, though not for a lack of looking. Nearly everyone else has found theirs, except for Garris. He's just too much of an oaf to focus properly.

No, my parents exist now only in my nightly reveries. In my 'containment anomalies,' as Cryptus refers to them. I hate that very term because it sounds so clinical and antiseptic. There's nothing wrong with dreaming about my parents. I welcome it.

What I wouldn't give to trade places *and* dream subjects with Anther: the object of his affections appear only in his dreams, but not in The Phoenix Experiment. I'd choose to have mine appear in The Phoenix Experiments rather than only in my dreams; in my waking life rather than in my sleep.

I glance over at the chairs next to me, briefly, and longing surges through me as I imagine my own parents here with me, today, *now.* I think of my mother's long, flowing hair, and my father's bristly brown beard. I imagine their smiles that were stolen from me, gone far too soon.

Thinking these thoughts, I close my eyes and attempt to conceal the fluid welling up in there, as Cryptus walks back to his control panel in a shielded room, preparing to monitor me.

He doesn't know my parents live on in my dreams. He, and I, want them to live in the tangible pseudo-reality that is the Phoenix Experiment. But, to date, I've been denied that, for whatever reason.

My only consolation is that the longer I go without contact, the closer I feel I'm drawing near to an inevitable first contact with them from the other side; beyond our world. I breathe, in and out, slowly, projecting my thoughts into a wistful, melancholy dreamscape, searching, searching, searching for them.

In the dark blackness of this room, I only know longing.

2: The Zephyr

No one sees it coming.

Suddenly, life changes, and The Zephyr is dead in space, floating helplessly across the diameter of the planet from The Origin.

The ship is listing, and oxygen is depleting rapidly from her exploded reserves. They show us pictures of the damage on the central news in our terminals. The Zephyr is identical in shape and mass to The Origin, but it's stationed across Earth's equator.

The two ships orbit as silent sentinels over our planet, spinning slowly around it in unending silence, never meeting.

A shuttle from The Zephyr is being prepared even now, and the death toll sits currently at 22 souls, including their Helmsman *and* Science Officer. The only adults left are two monitors, Chiefs Ashira Sarristo and Maridie Onyx, and their synthetic, Baryonnis Talicus. They are accompanying the 7 remaining girls, and are expected to arrive within two hours on the shuttle. I always find it comical when I hear synthetics have last names. They don't need them.

7 girls. There are 8 boys here. I wonder who will lose out, I think to myself. *Probably Dravin.*

Briefly I wonder why they had 32 people on board, whereas we have such a smaller number. We only have 15. Perhaps the girls required more experimentation because they're naturally more predisposed to emotion? Could that be why? Or were more males killed fighting the banshees, so there are less of us? I don't know. My thoughts are cut short as a new report comes in.

There is no hope for the Zephyr. It is on a buildup to detonation, and will explode within 30 minutes. Repair crews from Earth were en route to it but were turned back in orbit. Repair is futile.

I sit and listen to the news through the overhead coms. Helmsman Oculus is *not* happy, and he swears up and down through the broadcast, cussing so frequently the ceiling intercom turns blue. A group of us sits and listens to his angry tirade, laden with directives to maintain decorum and manners at all times. Like we didn't know to do that already.

We're all uncivilized miscreants here, Oculus, I think sarcastically to myself. His bristling tirade unfairly paints us as unruly apes itching for mayhem. "You are to do nothing untoward with our guests, and will treat them hospitably," he says. "They must be kept safe, by all of us. Failure to do so will result in confinement to quarters and loss of rec time for up to one week." I shudder at his threat, because it's certainly not hollow. Depriving us of rec time is Oculus' preferred method of punishment. Pretty sure everyone else shudders at the threat as well.

The girls, he says, are to remain aboard The Origin until such a time as they can be ferried over to their new ship. How long that will take, Oculus doesn't say, and probably doesn't know.

The Rubris is the only other G-class star freighter equipped for the Phoenix Experiments, and we can all see its location is out by the Trappist-1 system presently. It wouldn't be anywhere near us for at least a year. We don't know much about that ship, and questions posed by us boys have generally gone unanswered. A rumor persists that the Rubris had some kind of 'incident' onboard, and that's why it's so far away now. Banished, almost. It's been out there for years, but maybe whatever incident befell it has now been resolved. The unanswered questions pile high.

We will provide a temporary quarantine for the girls, our helmsman says. It's not safe down there for them yet; there are still far too many banshees all over the globe, and not enough Speakers to calm them. If the girls are anything like us, they haven't matured enough as Speakers to confront any of the creatures.

There's no way around it: they must avoid downtime, they need to continue with their own experiments here as well, and they've already been through enough trauma. Oculus stresses to us that they will *not* endure any more. His emphasis on *not* sounds like another subtle, intentional indictment of our character.

Our adult Chiefs, Marxim Bannitor and Hin Ambrosius, busy themselves below with rearranging Quadrant A, Floor 2 into the girls' temporary home away from home. There are connected pods, showers and living quarters there for guest staff, dignitaries (not like there are any left) and other visitors. It should do nicely.

I can't help but think, however, that Quadrant A, Floor 2 is about as far from our own dorms on Quadrant C, Subfloor 4D as you can get on this ship. What they *don't* know, however, is that Anther and I know about the maintenance passageways and ducting that connects everything together nicely for those with a penchant to snoop around. Anther and I have such a penchant, and as he gawks at me now, I can read that penchant all over his face. We'll have a good view of their showers, I'm sure.

I glance around wide-eyed at our guys. We're all gathered in the cafeteria, listening to the announcement.

Ranshay looks at me petrified as if the very word *girls* is a curse-word. He obviously wonders if it means the same as *banshees*. Ranshay is in for a sizeable surprise.

Garris smiles oafishly and looks like he's already mentally preparing to step up his flirting game.

Anther's jaw has dropped so low I presume he'll split at the ears. I watch him momentarily and figure he's got to shower and use deodorant if he's going to stand any kind of chance with them.

Venthix just stares at the overhead com, looking to be in the throes of fear. For the first time I wonder if he's gay; threatened by the incoming influx of X chromosomes.

Martos looks at us and nods with a massive crap-eating grin, ready to round up all the ladies for himself. But we all know he'll tire and pass out before he even has the energy to say hello to one of them.

At 8 years old, Dravin is the youngest of us. They practically snatched him up on his birthday. I don't even know if he fully understood where he was going or what he would be doing there. I swear they offered him milk and cookies and he just up and boarded their shuttle, no questions asked. He doesn't really understand the big deal about the girls coming; he sits off to the side of us, drawing a few monsters battling on a clean sheet of white paper as we listen.

And then, there's Finorin, or just 'Orin,' as we call him. He's the oldest, and he's well-built and rugged. He's only a few weeks shy of his 18th birthday, at which point he'll be released back to Earth. I have no knowledge of how well he's done in here, if he's reconnected, if he's ready to go 'save the world,' as we jokingly call it. He's a closed book. We'll see. He definitely has the muscles for it. If his Speaking ability matches his muscles, the banshees are done for.

Orin is an adult, practically, and I find myself watching him and hoping all the girls don't fall head over heels in love with his irritating man-pecs.

Anytime we think of the 'release,' it suggests to us that we've been nothing more than prisoners here this whole time, but that's not exactly true. It's a bittersweet graduation; we'll be released back to Earth and on our own to try to commune with our dearly departed in our own way, free from the help of The Origin. It's an unspoken truth that none of us wants our release. It's much safer in here. But we were conscripted, right? We chose The Origin. That means we're eventually going to have to be soldiers. So be it.

I glance over at Anther again. He can't contain his smile, and for a second I wonder if the mad hope steals through him that one of the girls might resemble the otherworldly girl of his dreams.

I shake my head at him.

He just smiles, and his grin is curved upward in unquenchably obvious hope.

I was right.

Shattered debris and particles zip by below us, circling the Earth in their orbit. Remnants of the exploded Zephyr, they now scream dangerously across the atmosphere, skimming and burning up. Several trillion dollars of Earth's capital, invested into that ship, now a waste.

Thankfully, we're high above the debris. The fragments pass us well before the Shuttlecraft Avalon arrives, with its precious cargo that all the boys are so excited about. Me, I'm not ambivalent; just feeling melancholy about the whole affair.

I had barely gotten out of my experiment when the news struck. It was sad news to begin with, but when you add the fact that I *still* didn't find my parents in there, it was a recipe for depression. I left Cryptus' office without saying goodbye. He was wordless as I passed him by glumly.

Now I stand on the observation deck with the rest of the gang. We stare wistfully out into the void as the Avalon approaches, a tiny glittering speck against the endless black ink of limitless space, preparing to dock with The Origin.

I glance around me, staring at my fellow Y-chromosomal shipmates. They are all practically salivating. An image flashes through my mind of some old nature show with an ibex swimming through a pond in Africa as wild dogs patrol the shore, waiting for it to emerge so they can feast. I roll my eyes. Have these wild dogs beside me no dignity?

"You guys are terrible," I say. "Give me a break." Two out of the seven of them look at me questioningly. Ranshay is one, only because he's trying to decipher what I said and translate it. The others don't take their eyes off the approaching shuttle. "These girls' ship just exploded and killed 22 of their own shipmates," I add, nodding out in space toward the Avalon. "Show a little class and stow your dinner napkins."

The Avalon is within fifty feet of The Origin, commencing docking maneuvers.

"Speak for yourself, Jax," Martos grunts. "I can't wait to meet 'em." He licked his lips. *Wild dog.*

"Please," I grunt back. "You'll be asleep before they even open the airlock."

The others chuckle at our interchange, but none of them is as heartless as Martos in dismissing the girls' recent trauma.

Anther presses himself up against the glass, trying to peek around the edge of our ship as the stern of the shuttle is lost from view. His hot breath fogs up the window and his fingers leave swirling impressions. A klaxon suddenly sounds throughout the ship and First Officer Mirabay's voice barks through. "Shuttle Avalon docking now. All crew prepare to receive the new arrivals."

Before we can say *new arrivals*, the eight of us are running to the cubeports, repeatedly slamming palms against the buttons and issuing orders to Phiria to summon one. The Origin's AI presence apologizes in an artificially heartfelt manner, providing an estimated time of arrival that far outlasts teenage patience.

It's no use. The display shows both of the cubeports to be in the next quadrant over. They won't get here in time, much less get us *there* in time. We abandon the cubeports and race to the stairwell, thundering down the stairs, most of us giggling like hooligans, whooping and hollering in anticipation.

"Settle down, midgets," shouts Orin. "Shut it! You don't want Oculus or Mirabay to hear us, do you?" We settle down and slow our pace, though by now I'm sure that Cryptus is already there, and he for *sure* has heard us. He's constantly connected wirelessly to Phiria anyway.

The docking bay draws near. We arrive on its floor, panting and with hearts a'flutter, and not just due to the exertion. I have to confess that I'm growing more excited the nearer we draw to the loading dock… *and the girls.* I want to meet them as well.

Orin slowly opens the door a hair, peeking through to get a lay of the land. Oculus and Mirabay stand there at the end of the shuttle hatch. Someone elbows me. I turn and see Anther smiling like an orangutan. His eyebrows flick up in anticipation. I shake my head.

Orin motions to us that he's going to open the door. He holds his finger to his lips as we nod in understanding. He playfully swoops his hand through his hair and sniffs his armpit to check his readiness, then frowns. So do we, because he stinks as much as Garris does. I decide that his stinkiness will work in my favor in attracting the girls to myself.

We silently enter through the stair doors, with class and military decorum. Oculus is suddenly aware of us and turns, nodding. He points for us to stand off to the side and wait. Cryptus had already turned and is watching the stairwell door as it opens, aware of our presence. He eyes us analytically.

Dull concussions and mechanical whirring sound from beyond as the shuttle latches onto The Origin. The clamps connect. Air hisses through joints and crevices. Signal lights on the wall change from red to green. Phiria announces a successful dock.

My heart skips a beat. I swallow. Suddenly, the hatch expands outward in a retracting pointed star pattern, and…

…there they are.

Seven girls are boarding our ship, right in front of all of us.

I see at least three of them right away, and at least one adult lingering behind them as they line up to disembark. Their outfits are strange, like ours but, fittingly, more feminine, accentuating their curves and revealing lower necklines. I have no objection to this. The colors of their uniforms are different as well, more pastel. Their silver nameplates glisten like ours do. Their appearance takes on a dreamy, glossy hue, almost as through a vignette. We all watch in awe, our hands clasped behind our backs, staring eagerly yet trying to remain stoic and dignified.

Girls are here.

"And this," Oculus says in almost a warning tone, "is Ensign Jax Hutson." Oculus has introduced everyone else, ending with me. The girls study us, nodding through their shell-shocked ordeal. They're not studying us as much as we're studying them, I guarantee it. My stomach is fluttering with a strange pandemonium of butterflies throughout.

Strangely, I'm fighting the urge to pee. I had forgotten to do so between my time with Cryptus and meeting the girls, and now I'm ready to burst. My nerves being on fire isn't helping. One of the girls, a long-haired red-head named Alaris, is drop-dead gorgeous, with eyes as colorful and shimmering as a nebula.

I glance over at Anther – and Martos – sidelong to see who they're eyeballing. I try to triangulate their view and ensure that neither of them are checking out my girl.

Wait, what?

But Alaris is beautiful, and that's that. So, I said *my girl*, and I meant it. It's during that thought that I see a faint smile creep across her lips as her eyes connect with mine, and I wonder if she's perceiving my thoughts, perhaps even feeling the same.

Out here amongst the stars, hope is essential.

I find myself smiling at her, and a swell of emotion wells up in me as I drink in her beauty.

Stop being a wild dog, I say to myself, just before Helmsman Oculus clears his throat.

"Chiefs Sarristo and Onyx," he says, "these are our Chiefs, Marxim Bannitor and Hin Ambrosius. Our ships' functionality should be fairly identical to yours. Phiria is here as well. Say hello, Phiria," he says, turning and looking up.

Our AI sounds out from above. "Welcome, passengers and crew of The Zephyr. My sincerest condolences on your recent losses," she finishes in a glum, empathetic tone.

In my heart I can't help but wonder if she means the 22 human souls lost, or the loss of a fellow ship with her own presence onboard. But that would imply *feeling*, and AI can only produce a facsimile of feeling. Just like Phiria is doing now.

Nonetheless, it resonates. The girls smile nervously and nod in thanks.

Oculus smiles. "Our synthetic, Mr. Stygius Cryptus, is here to ensure that your Phoenix experiments continue unhindered, and he will bring you up to speed."

Cryptus nods and musters an expression that might be loosely labeled a smile.

"Cryptus has been with us from the beginning, and he's tremendously talented with his work," Oculus continues. "Our Chiefs here will show you to your quarters. Quadrant A, three floors down from us, on Subfloor 3. The boys here are stationed on Subfloor 4D in their own quadrant. You'll have everything you need. Please join us for dinner this evening at 1800 hours in the mess hall," he finishes with a stern smile. It's not a request. I find that utterly odd. We haven't seen girls in years, and undoubtedly they haven't seen boys. *We're a bunch of hormone-crazed angst-ridden teens, and you throw us in the mix together? Didn't you want us focused? Aren't there rules against intermingling?*

Perhaps he's just trying to be a gentleman. We definitely don't want to turn a cold shoulder to our fellow humans who have not only been bereaved of their families, but then deprived of their shipmates as well. A little empathy goes a long way, even if it's over a rule-bending dinner.

I quickly scan the other guys' faces beside me. Brimming with hormones and unrestrainedly raucous before, they're all now equally as placid and tame as me, caught between trying to be a gentleman and trying to stay in compliance with Oculus' edict and the threat of losing rec. And *none* of them seems to be worried about the same thing that I am.

Wild dogs tamed.

I *really* have to pee.

Alaris smiles at me. The pressure fades as I smile back. She only has eyes for me. I hope the others notice.

"Did you see Miritia?!" Orin exclaims as we walk back to our quarters to prepare for dinner. There is talk among more than a few of them that they will have a second shower and spruce themselves up. "She is *fine*. That girl's gotta be 17 or 18, right? She's amazing!" He shakes his head in blissful incredulity as we stroll.

"Haha, Orin's got it bad," Martos teases. "She's a looker, for sure, buddy. For me, I really like Skarbé. What kinda name is that anyway, Dutch? Whoo!"

"It might be!" Orin says. "You can have her, bro. I call dibs on Miritia," he says, proudly.

"You can't call 'dibs' on a *girl*, Orin," Anther corrects him with a smile. "They're not, well, 'dibsable,' right? It's not like you're shopping for groceries."

"What the heck are *groceries*?" Orin asks annoyedly. "And who cares, stop talking! I'm trying to think about Miritia," he says in a wistful stupor. I'm just glad he didn't choose Alaris.

But then Anther speaks up.

"Man, did you guys see that red-head? She's freakin' gorgeous!" he exclaims. "What's her name?"

Spoke too soon.

"Alaris," little Dravin pipes up disinterestedly. I flinch, and look over at Anther, trying to conceal a glare. This is where I figure the best thing to do would be to employ a little reverse psychology on him.

"*Alaris?*" I ask with a sneer. "Gross. She was like the ugliest one out of all of them." Some of the guys laugh at my appraisal. Anther's smile fades. "You picked *her?*"

Anther's eyes flick away from me for a moment, unsure of what to say. His mouth moves without words as he tries to summon up a response. "Yeah," he defends. "I think she's cool. So?" he offers, rather mournfully.

I click my tongue and sneer at him in disapproval, pretending that he's insane in order to maintain my highly standoffish and very fake stance. I roll my eyes in disgust at him, and quickly look the other way while gritting my teeth.

"Yeah," Venthix says, "she was the best one of all of them, I think." *Okay, fine, confirmation that he's not gay. Or… maybe he's just trying to fit in. But also, frustrating.*

Orin chuckles in disagreement and shakes his head vigorously, laughing. "Seriously."

I start to feel a defensive roiling in my gut. I have to act fast.

"Yeah, I agree," chimes in Martos. "I think Alaris is the best."

"Totally," Garris the Neanderthal oaf agrees.

Ranshay says nothing; his eyes simply bounce back and forth between all of us like a wicked ping-pong match, not that he's ever played it, much less ever will. I watch as everyone who voiced that they like Alaris exchange approving glances between each other, and all I can do is humbly acknowledge that I'm now outnumbered as a contender.

As for myself, I'm determined to not allow the setback of the other guys' attraction to Alaris to become a prolonged one. In the back of my mind, I begin strategizing on ways to divert their attention.

But dammit, I think to myself, *if my ploy didn't backfire spectacularly.*

I just didn't see that coming.

3: The Tension

We haven't seen them, and I wonder why.

The girls have been here for 48 hours now. Following dinner, they were whisked away by their two female Chiefs, who were to then consult with Cryptus about the continuation of their experiments.

Dinner was fine, but we were all chagrined to find that Oculus had positioned himself, Cryptus, and our chiefs across from their girls, and positioned their chiefs across from us boys. So, each ship's crew was on separate sides of the table, and the boys were shifted down from the girls. I caught a sidelong smile from Oculus when he noticed our disappointment at this. *Jerk.*

Not like any of us would have been brave enough to pose any questions to the girls anyway. How do you even talk to a girl, much less one that you're actually interested in? I don't know. I don't think the other guys do either.

Be that as it may, I managed to catch a few stray glances my way from Alaris. She was definitely checking me out. One time she even blushed and looked away. Cryptus asked me to share my own appraisal of The Origin's Phoenix experiments, and it sure looked like she was listening to me intently. When I finished, she smiled at me, but my shipmates did not. I scanned their faces. They were jealous that she obviously liked me. Haha. Revenge is a dish that is best served cold. *How's it taste, fellas? The hot girl picked me. Not you. Me.*

Orin seemed to be the only one unfazed; he was, after all, interested in Miritia, and left Alaris to me. That helped.

As distracted by Alaris' beauty as I was, I was also listening. At one point, Cryptus started in on some kind of oration about getting our planet back. It was actually quite moving. So, try as I might to focus on Alaris and return the exchanges of smiles, I couldn't focus on her much for the rest of dinner.

Cryptus has a point. I know why I am here, and I know the deep burning drive within me comes from a longing to see my parents again. I have to become an effective Speaker. We Speakers – we *all of us* – have to reclaim our planet, and these girls deserve to be a part of that success as well. To that end, we aren't here to perfect our pair bonding. We have to focus. All things in due time.

Earth, we all know, has a timeline. The natural resources will always grow. Trees will bloom again and bear fruit. Gardens will produce vegetation. The sun still shines and the rain still falls. But our structures are relatively unmanned, our facilities are overgrown with brambles and creepers, and it's a ghost town down there due to all those dang banshees. We have to reclaim the Earth! People are dying. There can be no interruption. The calamity with The Zephyr is a setback, we all concur, but we are determined to maintain our focus, and not allow the setback to become a prolonged one. Oculus is right.

> *The enemy below doth sleepeth not*
> *Nor frets the day when mankind bought*
> *Their means to calm,*
> *their soothing balm*
> *The Phoenix Experiments mean naught*

> *So press on, wayward foolish mortal*
> *Continue on toward thy vain portal*
> *We lie here, waited,*
> *our breaths bated*
> *Prepared to at thy deaths give chortle*

It's time for my experiment, so I get ready to check in with Cryptus. Chow time over, I'm dressed and ready, almost to the nines today because there are now girls on our ship. I dab on a bit of cologne for the first time in ages. And as I pass all of the other guys, I catch a whiff that they've done the same. Even little Dravin smells like a bed of roses. They must have held him down and slathered him. Girls aren't even on his radar yet. Sure wish there were girls here more often; we all smell pretty hideous otherwise.

Though we're kept apart, there is only one Phoenix lab on this whole ship. I find that very odd considering how big this ship is, how savage the banshees are, and how many people have died. But, in truth, there's also only one synthetic. As effective as he is, Cryptus is not omnipresent; he can't be in multiple places at once.

Nonetheless, if we were to receive a new influx of orphans, we would definitely need more labs. The Origin seems so bloated and overspaced… like a vast aquarium established for a single school of minnows. There has to be a reason. I understand, however, that shuttles are limited, and firing up a shuttle on Earth is a recipe for disaster, as it's sounding the dinner gong for banshees. They can't just whisk a shuttle our way each time; they have to strategize and send them up in bulk, secretively, when the banshees are subdued or distracted… or on the other side of the world.

The girls' synthetic – I remember her name is Baryonnis Talicus – is nowhere to be found, but the girls assure me she is remaining below to serve them and provide educational services. I wonder if she and Cryptus have spoken. I assume there is some desire on each of their parts to do so. But knowing them, they're both AI; they could simply plug into terminals at various points throughout The Origin and commune with each other remotely through Phiria. Strange. Eerie. *Whatever; it's their way,* I think.

I decide to ponder that more later.

For now, I realize that I may actually run into one of the girls at the lab, passing each other like ships in the night. The boys all have hourlong shifts every day; Cryptus informs us, however, that for the time being our schedules have been reassigned to every *other* day, to accommodate the girls. Cryptus will alternate between genders and accommodate us equally. I take no umbrage with this; *I'm not finding my parents in there anyway,* I think to myself, glumly.

There's a palpable tension in the air. There has been ever since the girls arrived. Even though The Origin is vast, our population goes from 14 to 25 just like that. A horrific thought passes through me: what if something tragic happens with The Rubris as well, on its way to us? We'd be the only ship left! Surely, they couldn't transfer everyone aboard this ship. We'd all be sardines in a tiny, tin can, overloaded and cramped beyond belief. And if there were any more girls, us wild dogs would probably detonate from overstimulation.

Besides, whatever happened to them in the first place? I wonder.

In the meantime, it's inescapable: we're all truly a bit more on edge, quick to quibble over the stupidest minutiae.

Anther and I got in a heated argument last night over which kind of banshee is the worst. I maintained that the scurriers are the worst, because there's no escape, and they can get you while you sleep. He argued back that, no, the plodders are the worst, because they're so large, they can cover more ground and literally stomp you into goo. And there are rumors of creatures more terrifying than either of these, but they have no name.

I see his point, but I don't agree with him, and then our volume rose as we were both shouting over each other, fangs bared. Thankfully, Orin stepped in and knocked our heads together. But Anther and I didn't speak over dinner as a result.

It's like all of our hormones are on the fritz, amplified and hypersexualized.

Wild dogs.

Venthix and Martos actually got into a fight. It was ridiculous. We laughed as they pummeled each other. Venthix landed a right hook that sent Martos sprawling. The venomous look that Martos gave him once he collected himself was priceless. I'd pay good credits to get it framed and hang it on my wall. It got so violent and so loud that Oculus came in, and we shut right up and stood at attention. Martos and Venthix stood there bleeding, apologizing their asses off. Cryptus then came in and cleaned them up, sterilizing their wounds and applying salve. They both lost out on rec time for two days straight, and have to pen a research paper on the history of banshees. Sucks to be them.

Last night I had a dream, and not a pleasant one. *Yes,* I got to meet my parents in it – and I thank the serum for that – but my dream was *flooded* with banshees, and I was deathly afraid, flitting from shadow to shadow. I was in some abandoned warehouse on Earth, and they were all shrieking outside. I just knew at any minute they would find me and shriek into my soul until I have a coronary. That's exactly how my parents died. A plodder got my mom and a scurrier got my dad. They didn't stand a chance. That awful dream sees me waking up and screaming. Phiria registered my emotional strain immediately.

"Good early morning, Jax," she greeted me calmly. I glanced at the clock. 0135 hours in the morning. "Is everything okay? Would you like a sedative infusion with your serum?"

I shook my head. "No, thank you, Phiria. I'm fine. Just a bad dream."

"No problem," she replied warmly. "According to Regulation 35B2, Section H, please ensure that if your dream pertains to your parents, that you file the appropriate Containment Anomaly Repor-"

"Yes, yes, I know, Phiria. Thanks," I dismissed her. It was too early for regulations.

"My pleasure." She silenced.

Phiria is sweet but annoying. A little too saccharin and cheery for my taste. There's something so artificial about cheery. We don't live in a cheery environment, nor is Earth in a state of cheer at the moment. We're all bracing and holding on, trying to jumpstart healing.

The banshees are determined to deny us that.

Fortune favors the foolhardy. I quickly make my way to Cryptus' lab and, wonder of wonders, there are two girls there. One of them is in Cryptus' office waiting for their turn to go through Phoenix. Another is already in the chair and synced up. Just my luck, neither one is Alaris. *That's fine,* I think to myself. I'll acquaint myself with the two that *are* here. After all, no time like the present. Maybe they can tell Alaris how awesome I am when they report back.

They both look to be on the younger side. The one in the lab is the youngest of the girls who stepped off the Avalon and into our lives. She's asleep and hooked up. Cryptus monitors her astutely. The one sitting in front of me out here in Cryptus' foyer looks to be just a bit older. She smiles a wide, toothy grin at me and perks up, bobbing slightly. Her skinny arms are delicate and fair, and her blonde hair is tied into two equal-sized braids close to her head, running down her neck into silver clasps.

"Hi, I'm Jax," I say, sticking out my hand. "Jax Hutson."

The girl accepts it and shakes it, greeting me in turn. "Omnias," she says. "Omnias Prasuth. Good to be aboard your ship. It's beautiful. I've been on The Zephyr for five years. I'm 13. How about you? How old are you?"

Wow. Precocious, I think to myself. "Uh, nice to meet you, Omnias. I'm 14. Been here for five years. Nice to meet you. Who's that in there?" I ask, nodding into the lab.

"That's Zaris Sharibian, my friend. She's only 11." Her smile fades a bit, as if she's miffed that I'm inquiring about her friend. Little does she know I'm interested in Alaris, and *I'm* slightly miffed that *she's* not here. "Zaris is doing her Phoenix session right now."

"Uh, yes, I see that," I say, sitting down across from her, and then an awkward silence follows as she bites her lip and looks around. "We do them too," I add, finally, punctuating the silence.

"Neat. I'm next," she says, beaming, and then her head cocks to the left. "Is it true you guys have the same crappy food goo here? *Please* tell me there's lobster!" She practically leans forward from her bench toward me, eyebrows up as she pleads.

My head cocks in turn. "Lobster? No, no lobster. We have the same crap, sorry. I assume you're talking about *BioPrime.* Pretty sure they have that on all the ships." I chuckle sheepishly at the stupidity of it, and can guess her upcoming reaction.

She scowls and slams her back against the leather rest behind her in a huff, sulking. "Oh… that… tasty… *BioPrime*," she says in a mumbled sing-songy caricature of the commercial jingle for our revolting food paste. "Barf."

I chuckle. "Barf indeed." *I was right.*

"You'd think with all the research we're helping them do, they'd budge an inch and give us a nice, juicy steak for once," she complains.

I don't tell Omnias that I thought the very same thing just a few days ago. A slab of the apparently delicious meat flashes through my mind, but the taste doesn't, because I just don't know what it's like. I shift nervously in my seat. "Steak would be nice. Have you ever had it?"

"Nope."

"Yeah, me neither."

"I saw you hanging with that one guy, is his name Anther? Anther Seeto, is it?"

"*Sec*-to," I say. "Yeah. He's alright," I say, sloughing off my best friend, the banshee argument still fresh in my mind, and wanting to get him back for liking Alaris. "Did you meet him?"

Omnias shakes her head. "Hmm-mmm, no. He just seems nice," she says, blushing.

Ahhh, now I get it, I think to myself. *I'm sure I can use this.*

I look around me quickly, as if scrounging for tools. "Uh, yeah, he's pretty cool, actually. I've known him for a long time. I can introduce you two, if you'd like?" I offer, because my name is apparently Helpy Helperton.

She blushes, and I've scored a victory, no matter how sinister. "Yeah! Sure. I mean, no rush, it would be cool, but not a big deal if it doesn't happen."

Sure. I believe that as much as I can throw it. Here is where I seek my leverage.

"I can do that, sure. He's a good guy. Hey! Since we're asking, do you know, uh, what's her name," -here I play dumb to score my first acting award- "*Alaris* very well? Is that her name? Alaris?" *Smooth. I'm good.*

"Uh," Omnias replies, "yeah, I could introduce you too. At chow time tonight, maybe? She's cool. I don't know her *really* well, I hang with Zaris more, but I can def-"

A loud bang emits from the chamber, and we both jerk out of our conversation, rising quickly and staring in through the observation window. Zaris has flinched and kicked in her subconscious. Her expression is a twisted knot of angst, and her breathing has quickened, mouth agape. We both glance over at Cryptus, who remains as emotionless as an equation, studying her with impartiality. We hear the EKG beep more frenetically, but then it slows.

I briefly wonder if he worries about her or *any* of us in there, and what he would do if we went into cardiac arrest or something drastic like that. Would he act just as dispassionately, staring at us coldly and waiting for us to stop being such a dramatic human?

The drama subsides, and we both sit back down.

"That was weird," Omnias grunts, her eyes flashing back and forth. "Does that happen a lot?"

I shrug. "No idea. Not sure. I don't know what 'that' even was. Probably just a bad dream or something."

"But the Phoenix isn't a dreamcycle. It's just a mental probe, right?" she asks, and I feel like I'm on the witness stand in some courtroom case being cross-examined.

"Yeah, I think that's right," I agree.

"So, she's not dreaming. She wasn't having a nightmare or anything like that. Those only happen in our sleep."

"You have nightmares on The Zephyr?" I ask her, curiously.

"*Had* them, yes. Our ship is toast. What, you don't have them here?"

"Well, we have the serum, and-"

"Ew! The what?"

I stare at her blankly, wondering why they didn't do it the same way over there. "The serum.

You know, the shot?" I raise my underarm to show her the port we all have implanted to receive the nightly serum injection. "To calm us, to enable us to dream, so that we're well-rested for our Phoenix experiments."

She just stares at me, gawking, as if this is the craziest thing she's ever heard. "You guys get a serum in order to dream? That's so weird."

"What, you guys just… dream? Without serum?"

"Stop saying *serum,*" she orders, flatly.

I can't reply because the EKG starts beeping frantically, intermittently. We both glance in through the window again to see Zaris flinch. And then flinch again. And then spasm and lurch.

In a mix of curiosity and worry, we both flash our eyes over to Cryptus, staring at her coldly through the observation window still, his face eerily underlit as his heavy-lidded eyes monitor her emotionlessly.

Zaris continues to flinch, and occasionally she thrashes her legs. Her face suddenly contorts into a clench of what looks like fear, and a deep, guttural sob wells up in her throat and bursts out into a roar of panic.

Before Omnias or I can say anything, Zaris' eyes open wide, and they're white as frost. Her mouth is utterly agape, and an unearthly throbbing moan emits from the cavern of her little mouth that defies her size. It's a low, barreling sound, a hellish sound, a demon-roar, loud as an engine in the sky but churned up from horrific depths of somewhere desperately macabre. She is momentarily frozen in that expression, and my flesh crawls as I watch her. Her eyes roll back in her head.

Zaris relents and closes her mouth once more. All is silent except for the constant beeps of the monitoring machinery.

Yet her EKG speeds up.

My thoughts go back to the girls' synthetic, Baryonnis Talicus. I wonder what she would do in this situation, and why she's not here!

We press our faces up to the window. Omnias cries out "Zaris! Mr. Stygius, help her!"

"Cryptus," I correct her, absentmindedly, but then the android jerks himself up from his desk and throws open the control room door. I pan my eyes back to Zaris. She is now convulsing. Her eyes flutter open, and her chest spasms in great heaps as her back arches reflexively and wincing cries of stuttered agony emit weakly from her. The android walks briskly over to her with something in his hand, and for a moment I wonder why he isn't running. He quickly bends down over her and presses the device in his hand to her temple. Zaris flinches. A loud pop is heard as a spark lights up the room.

Omnias and I flinch at the sight.

Suddenly, the third chair brightens as if lit from within by a white fire. Momentary, yes, like a giant spark, but nonetheless alarming. For a brief moment, there is a dim shape in that light, but it disappears. My jaw drops in fright as I witness it, but it's hard to take my eyes off Zaris. Something is truly wrong here!

In a reflex, I throw open the waiting room door and burst into the lab. Omnias follows right on my heels. "Cryptus, what's happ-"

With surprising deftness and volume, Cryptus spins on his heels and faces us, his eyes wide. "Go *baaaaack!*" he howls monstrously, pointing at us.

My feet stop short of Zaris' chair and I backpedal. Omnias collides with me. I hold her back, nodding at Cryptus. "Ye-yes, sir," I say, feebly, pushing Omnias behind me and back out into the waiting room. Cryptus does not turn around again toward Zaris until we're back in the lobby and the door lock clicks in front of us.

The EKG slows. Once more Cryptus presses the whatever-it-is against Zaris' temple. Once more the pop. The EKG slows even further and normalizes. Zaris' chest stops heaving, her face unclenches, her fists unball themselves, and she relaxes, her breathing slowing. Her head is now beaded with sweat, and as the crinkles slowly disappear from her face, she swallows deeply, as if willing herself to recover from a fear she never thought she would have to face.

It has been several hours. I am sitting now in D-Block with Anther. "I'm telling you," I maintain, "it was like Cryptus was doing something to her. I don't know what it was, but it felt sinister. I've never experienced anything like that before, and I've never heard of anyone else going through anything like it."

Anther just stares at me, for the moment completely forgetting our feud. "And what happened after that?"

"I don't know, man! We just bolted out of there and went back to our respective areas. And you found me here. I've just been here."

"Wait, didn't you have a session today?"

"Yeah, but I bolted! You think I want to be in there with Cryptus after he did that to that girl?"

"Did what to her?" Anther presses.

"I mean – you know what I mean. It *looked* like he was doing something. And I wasn't going to be next!"

"You think Cryptus is doing something to them in their sleep? Or to us?"

"Dude, I have no idea," I say, resigned to dwell in uncertainty. "It was just so weird and traumatic, watching her."

"Well, I did run into Omnias after that. She said you went back here. Oculus is letting us do rec together, but we have to behave of course. Martos and Venthix were *livid* when they heard that we get to rec with them. But Omnias said she was fine. I saw Zaris. Didn't talk to her, but she looked okay to me. Happy as a clam. I think Omnias likes me, by the way," he says, cocking an eye and a smile and completely jumping the tracks, deviating from our conversation.

"Stay focused."

"Anyway, Omnias said that she didn't want to talk to Zaris about it. It doesn't seem like Zaris remembers it anyway."

"Seriously? Like… amnesia? That didn't look like something you could just easily forget," I insist. "She was traumatized. Freaking bouncing off her lab chair. And the third chair…," I trail off.

Anther stares at me, waiting. "The third chair *what?*" He pauses, sizing me up and down.

I wait and think, trying to remember.

"What, dude? Spit it out!"

I shake my head. "I don't know. It was almost like… some kind of shape was suddenly in that chair. Like a presence or… or… something," I finish. "I don't know," I repeat. "It was just eerie as hell, dude."

Anther says nothing.

"I want to get another look at what that thing was that he used on Zaris. I've never seen it before, and he had it with him in the control room. I wonder if it was some kind of injector, or… or… shock device, or something."

"Dude, you're losin' it. You're mental," Anther blurts out in a near-laugh.

"It's not funny, Ant. I was really worried about that girl." I sigh. Anther doesn't say anything else, and I hope my concern resonates with him.

"Zaris looked okay though?" I finally ask him. I feel genuine concern for her, and would love to see her. Now I'm doubting myself, wondering if it was just some fluke. Cryptus has been at the helm of the Phoenix Experiments for all this time. There is no reason to assume ill of him based on one potential anomaly.

"As far as I could tell, but I don't really know her. But I'd like to get to know Omnias, if you know what I mean."

"Not Alaris?" I ask, mustering up my best look of dispassionate incredulity.

Anther tilts his head and glares at me under his brows. "Dude, you're a loser. Stop pretending like you don't like her. It's clear she likes you. Everyone knows it."

"What do you mean, everyone?"

"*Everyone*. From Orin down. Hell, even Ranshay knows it, and he doesn't even speak English," Anther growls. "It's fine. She's yours. I don't wanna compete with you. You're my best friend. I'll take Omnias. She's cute." He pauses, eyeing me. "But just know that if we *did* compete, I'd shred you."

A grin slowly molds my lips into an indefensible acceptance. "Sure you would."

"I would," he says. "Painfully. Decisively."

"Decisively, huh? Isn't that a big ten dollar word for a meathead like you?"

"Believe it, spitfire," he says, cockily.

It's then that I realize that he is the one who got me labeled as a spitfire; it's *also* then that I realize he's aware that I'm the one who labeled him as a meathead. We enter a calm truce at the realization.

So be it.

"Well, remind me not to compete with you. But scurriers *are* the worst," I jab, referring back to our argument.

Anther smiles and shakes his head.

The rest of the day goes by without a hitch.

However, I don't see Cryptus anywhere, and I wonder why.

4: The Lost

Three more uncertain days go by, slowly, it seems.

Oculus confirms that the Rubris is indeed en route, and we will provide safe haven for the girls until it gets here. We are all thrilled at this news, of course, because Phiria confirms that it will take The Rubris four-hundred and thirty-two days to reach us at present speed. That's over a year. The girls will be with us all that time, which is completely fine with us boys.

The Zephyr has completely disintegrated by now, its remnants pulverized by the crushing weight of space, its entrails spinning haphazardly, fated to burn up in Earth's diminishing atmosphere below. Its only artifacts are the girls, their chiefs and their synthetic who now live aboard The Origin.

Over the past three days I report twice to Cryptus' lab as scheduled, given the fact that I missed a day, as well as the fact that we're now sharing scheduling with the girls. Each time, Cryptus appears as though nothing happened with Zaris the other day. It's as if he doesn't remember. He is pleasant as a peach, and greets me enthusiastically in a saccharin tone. There is no mention of a blue pen.

"Ensign Hutson! So good to see you this fine morning," he greets me. I stare at him with an awkward confusion and obligatory nod as I pass by him into the chamber. "How did you sleep?" he asks in a sing-songy voice, over-inflecting to the point of nauseating. "Any containment anomalies last night?"

I shake my head. "No."

"Of course not. Most excellent. Glad to see that you are remaining focused. Shall we proceed?"

I just watch him, perhaps searching for a trace of telling guilt or some minute desire to explain the bizarre ordeal Zaris went through on his watch only a few days ago. Granted, I have not been here to witness the other lab sessions, but I can't help but wonder if any of the other girls – or boys – went through any similar ordeals.

I strap myself in as Cryptus retreats to the wall console and taps various controls. "We shall. Will you be using any new equipment this session?" I ask timidly, fearful of his response as I'm fully referencing the device that he used to 'pop' Zaris in the temple.

He turns to me, and his smile fades. "Please explain," he says, suddenly coldly, and his bulbous, heavy-lidded eyes study me until I hate him all over again. He slowly returns to my side, staring at me the entire time.

"I-I was just curious," I stammer, "if you've upgraded the equipment since last time."

He fixes his eyes on me as I wither in the heat of his glare. The synthetic slowly rotates his head around the lab, inviting me to do the same. "Ensign Hutson, you are free to survey my laboratory as you see fit. Please. Do you observe anything new in here?"

I slowly pull my eyes away from him, and a macabre dread washes over me that he's going to knock me out and pop me with that thing, whatever it was, once I look away. But he doesn't. And I don't see the device anywhere. Of course I don't. It's safely stowed in his viewing room. I determine silently to sneak a peek at it with Anther as soon as we can.

I want to sigh, but that would give me away. "No," I relent. "I was just curious." Now it's time to act, and put his suspicion to rest. "As you know I still haven't made contact with my parents. I was just hoping that this might be the time."

"And why might this now suddenly be the time?" he asks me, almost before I've finished speaking.

I watch him. *Maybe the direct approach wasn't the right one. I'll pivot and try humor now instead,* I think.

"Come on, Cryptus," I say with a smirk, "after all the times I've gone in, look at me. Maybe I stand a better chance of finding your *pen* than I do my parents. You prefer blue, right?" I stifle a manufactured giggle.

He just stares at me. The reference holds no meaning for him. "I'm sorry, I don't understand, Jax. What is this about a pen?"

A wave of uncertainty washes over me as I gawk at him. My smile fades. He doesn't remember the pen? How could he not remember the pen? Androids have a photographic memory and are constantly recording data. Surely he must be joking; there is *no* way he wouldn't remember it. I squint my eyes at the synthetic standing before me, looking him up and down. Is he malfunctioning? Did that device he used on Zaris pop something in his own circuitry and disrupt his memory modules?

I stutter. "No-nothing, Cryptus. It's fine," I say.

An awkward moment of impasse lingers between us as he studies me once more. I finally allow my expression to change, though behind my eyes I'm still thinking about Zaris, and what went wrong in her Phoenix experiment, and the part that Cryptus must have played in it. Suspicion eats me like a canker inside, but I have to stow it. I dig in my heels and just meet his eyes, carefully avoiding a guilty visage.

Cryptus stands uncomfortably close to me and studies me. I'm grateful for the barrier of flesh and bone and independence that prevents him from reading my thoughts.

He finally retreats, wordlessly, and I breathe easy once more. He is *so* creepy.

Before too long I'm hooked up and ready to go, the confrontation now only a distant memory. *Pens, schmens.* I don't care anymore. I don't want to find a pen for Stygius Cryptus. I never did.

I only want to find my parents again.

Cryptus retreats to the control room.

Cue the white noise.

Cue the deep throbbing.

I'm told stories by Cryptus now and then about how, long ago, parents used to employ white noise on babies simply by driving them around in cars. Down there on earth, the road noise would be too much for the babies to handle. It was overwhelmingly peaceful, he said, and the babies would fall fast asleep from the lulling effect.

Cryptus says that the white noise and throbbing in here is not all that different, really; it's effusive, undulating, pulsating, overwhelming, and ultimately effective even on older humans such as myself. When he initially told me that prior to my very first Phoenix experiment, my initial thought was *well, we'll just see about that.*

How wrong I was. Jax Hutson doesn't stand a chance against the white noise. No one does.

Before too long, I enter a state just south of what could be called consciousness, and the sounds take me.

I am wandering through an old memory. I think I am 5 years old, and the trappings and layout of our old house call out to me from the recesses of my heart. I don't know them anymore, of course, because it's been several years, and the planet seems light years away from me now, even though it slowly rolls by below The Origin every single day of my now life. My guess is I'm in our old living room; there are plush couches and chairs, and the antiseptic white cleanness of the room suggests a healthy comfort that I might have once enjoyed. An overly large display screen is mounted on the wall, and sconces dot the surrounding walls, projecting a warm blue torch-like illumination for accent lighting.

Things are hazy; less clear than the here and now aboard our ship, but they retain a level of clarity that is amplified by the yearning in my heart to recall them clearly. Tilted frames hang along the wall, revealing portrait sessions with my family that I have no memory of. Small, nondescript toys litter the floors of our home, but I can't make them out. They hold no emotional weight for me anymore, and I don't remember what weight they might have held anyway.

A small, furry figure scampers past me, and I jump, startled. It doesn't heed me. I'm not really there anyway; it knows it, and I know it. It's a poodle, and a brief surge of disdain courses through me. Maybe I didn't like it when I was a boy. Maybe I don't like poodles. I don't know. It scampers by me on its way to somewhere else in our home.

Dim, blurry light filters in through the windows across a corridor leading to what I guess must be the living quarters. As I draw near, a smaller room en route makes me crane my head and peer inside it.

I am now staring at my old bedroom, and I know it. There are various caricatures of a superheroic figure dotting the room, the bed comforter, the dresser, the end table light, but I don't know who it is.

There are no more superheroes, anyway.

I struggle to make out the numerous artifacts and relics of a bygone age composing the character of my old bedroom. I have no memory of the things in here, although I vaguely recall *being* here. Sleeping here. Playing here. A scattershot flicker of a memory shoots through my mind of circling up under that superhero comforter, my dad perched next to me, one heavy leg hanging off of my bed as he reads me a bedtime story. I don't remember the story.

I'm an impartial observer here; removed enough to be unbiased, but emotion struggles to surface, to connect with *something* here, to make it more real and tangible in my memory. It was so long ago: nine years, to be exact, and a lifetime away.

Friggin' banshees, I think to myself, as I decide to just move on down the hall. Longing fills me to be here again, to live here, to have peace here. To have my parents here. Longing that I must subdue and repress. *No, not 'repress,'* I tell myself. *Make peace with.* Make peace with in order to have closure, and emerge stronger. *That's the whole reason I'm in here,* I remind myself.

Just as I grab the doorframe and prepare to tug myself away from the faded memories and head back toward my parents' room, I hear it.

It's different than the undulation of the white noise. It's some kind of shrill sound, a call of some kind, but there are words in it. I can't make it out. My ears strain, both in life and in the Phoenix Experiment, and I wonder, briefly, if Cryptus is aware of what I'm hearing.

Of course he is, though. That's what he does. That's all he does. Monitors all of it. Sees and hears everything, transmitted by the electrodes and probes on and in me, sending near-perfect 3D display representations of all that I'm witnessing and experiencing, in 24K clarity, back to his control room. I wonder what he thinks he heard just now as well.

I crane my head and look back over my shoulder. The dog bounds past me again, heading back the way we both just came. For just a moment, it stops, looks back toward my parents' bedroom, and sniffs, almost as if it detects some faint, ethereal presence here. Me: a spiritual bedouin making my way through this luminescent reverie. We're both connected somehow, though completely sundered.

I follow the dog toward the front door, slowly, and a name jumps out at me, though I don't know why, nor where it came from. *Poppy*? I'm guessing that's the dog's name, because the moment I think of it, it stops, turns back, and cranes its neck for a moment, cocking an ear. Realizing it was nothing more than a temporary anomaly, it lets out something akin to a dismissive sneeze, and then carries on once more.

I continue to follow Poppy.

There it is again. The noise. It's growing louder. Amidst the tendrils of sound clawing at me, something is grasping for purchase in my ears and brain. It's higher-pitched, and it sounds like it's coming from outside.

Poppy is facing the main door to our home. I regard it curiously as it sits there, patient, wagging its little popcorn tail, its eyes glued to the door.

Compulsion seizes me, and I suddenly find myself moving swiftly toward the door, intent on deciphering the sound. Morning light streams through the living room windows, and the blue torches flicker briefly as if a light breeze steals through.

I'm almost to the door.

Poppy, sensing me, scampers out of the way and retreats into the living room. The chanting again, eerily calm, swamped in dreamy reverberation, pulses around me:

> *O'er the moors the memories flee*
> *What once was is ne'er to be*
> > *Darkness reigns,*
> > *fear regains*
> *And vanity blanketeth land and sea*

> *Unrequited listless calls*
> *Go unanswered in the halls*
> > *Of unmet longs*
> > *and far-felt wrongs*
> *A testament to deathly falls*

I grab the door handle. All is calm, even the chanting. Poppy turns and skitters further back, and I don't know why. I turn the handle.

With violent force, the door is suddenly thrown wide open, and the screaming erupts. I know that scream! We're trained to recognize it. A thunderous heat wave blasts over me, scorching my skin as I shield my face. Wind buffets me. Fires rage outside: hungry flames of yellow and amber and orange and white, blowing and wavering and seeking to consume me.

Poppy yelps and bolts.

But it's the scream. It's not the howling wind racing over me that I fear. It's that scream that doesn't abate, and grows in intensity as it pitches ever upward in a haunting cry. The cry is composed of notes intended to shatter a human skeleton, piercing muscles with hissing tones that freeze your sinews in horror. Were I flesh and bone in here, it would do just that.

It's the cry of a banshee. This one seems different, somehow: louder, more toxic, more lethal.

I can't see it, but it's there, and there are perhaps more than one outside the relative calm of my home. They're searching for me, and I feel their prying eyes, hungry to devour my yearning and suck away my life force through the channel of my heart's deep longing.

Darkness reigns, fear regains...

But then, once more, permeating that scream, I hear it. I hear it! It's a shrill voice, trying desperately to punch through the clatter. It's nigh on impossible; a banshee's monstrous cry is indomitable.

I know now there are many, and they are hunting for me. But I, too, am a hunter, and I find myself now hunting for that voice. I can still hear it!

I decide to be strong. I steel myself.

What once was is ne'er to be.

I'm okay with it. I'm okay with not living here and not knowing these toys and not remembering these framed portraits. I'm okay with my parents not being here. What once was is not to be.

Not today, banshees. Not today.

I ball my hands into fists, and lower them to my sides, facing the onslaught of noise pressing against me, seeking to claw its way into my heart. I stare it down, unflinching, my hair blowing in the wind.

I hear the shrill voice. It's growing.

The flames lessen. I recognize them for what they are: just an illusion. I breathe deeply and try to focus on the voice. It's still there. Calling. What is it saying? "Back! Back!" Is that what it's saying? Is someone being attacked by the banshee and they're resisting, bravely, though futily? Only a Speaker can banish a banshee.

For a moment I wonder what I look like as I lie there on the chamber, and if Cryptus is watching me intently, or fingering some mysterious device and preparing to press it to my temples. I dismiss this thought and resume my focus.

Breathe, Jax. You got this.

I slowly walk outside, into the flames. They ebb and flicker into tiny tongues, deprived of their intensity. Thick, gray smoke eddies in the air.

The wind calms into bursts of a whisper.

The banshee screams seem to recede into an unguessable distance.

But the voice remains. I hear it clearly now, slowly emerging through the fog and sludge of noise, coalescing into clarity as the words become concrete, permeating the intangible and taking shape in my ears and mind.

Unrequited listless calls...

With astonishing clarity, as the hubbub dissipates all around me and calm seeps out from the house, flowing down the streets of the neighborhood, drowning all the tumult in peace, I hear it clearly now.

I was wrong. It wasn't "Back! Back!"

Jax! Jax!

And then, with waves of longing rippling down my skin, I see them. Two figures, emerging from the wisps of lingering fire-smoke, running down the street, on a torrent of emotion, carried by their hearts, racing toward me.

I recognize them instantly as my eyes begin to water and my heart throbs in a perfect balance of pain and purity. My skin tingles, and sobs emerge from me. I can't contain them. I am engulfed in a flood of yearning.

Her hair is blowing deftly in the wind, streaming behind her, bouncing off her jacket as she draws near.

His thick legs thunder beneath him as his feet pound the pavement, his bushy beard drenched with beads of sweat and saliva.

They reach for me.

And I reach for them, my eyes now streaming tears and my mouth calling out in unbridled desire and delight!

"Mom! Dad!"

My parents. I see them! My feet suddenly and swiftly carry me of their own accord, racing down the street toward them as our paths converge, my heart bursting with joy by the respite from overwhelming longing.

I weep…

…and the fires around me roar back to life.

I weep. My heart yearns.

It's everything I can do to keep from plunging headlong into this dream state forever… if only I could feel their embrace one more time.

The wind rises again to a deafening cacophony.

I weep. My heart yearns. I reach out.

It's no use. Futility and vanity rise up like a smoking haze, screening me off from them and denying my heart what it's burned for, for five years now.

The banshee screams rip through the skies and hammer us hard, smelling my yearning and licking its lips at my heart's cry. All three of us are thrown to the ground as the sound murders our desire and lays waste to our intentions.

And vanity blanketeth land and sea…

And then, just as I reach for them again, I feel a pressure in my temple, and a loud pop sounds.

Just like that, it seems that five more despondent years go by, slowly.

5: The Contact

My heart is in my throat, and I'm sobbing hard.

"Curse you, Stygius Cryptus, why did you bring me out?! *Why?!* Curse you!" I rail at him. "I found them, I *finally* found them, and you yank me out? How *dare* you!" I scream at him. His remorseless face is a blank slate as he stands before me, a strange device in his hand.

My temple throbs as I look at it. He obviously used it on me: the device he popped Zaris with. A surge of adrenaline roars through me, blinding my eyes with red rage, as tears stream down my face and my lip quivers. I rush at him and grab his lapels, shaking him. "Why?! Why, Cryptus, why?!" I rattle him with each fierce scream.

"Ensign Hutson, your reaction is not atypical for a first encounter with your parents. I assure you-"

"Atypical? Go to hell, Cryptus! You *knew* I was searching for them and would give *anything* to hold them again! You knew!" He blurs before me while my eyes fill with tears as I howl.

"Jax, I am instructing you to release me. I-"

"No! You don't instruct me! You're nothing! You're a useless, dumb synthetic who can't even-"

"Ensign Jax Hutson, *release* me." He commands it robotically, mechanically, with all the emotion of a coat hanger.

"No! You *knew* I desperately needed to see them! You-"

Without a word, the device in his hand is released, and it hovers silently to a table behind him, returning to a black charging dock. Two iron grips laden with artificial hair follicles seize my wrists and wrench my fingers from his lapels. My eyes widen. With dizzying speed, he recoils and then launches a punch dead center into my chest. I fly backward and tumble to the ground, my head colliding with a stainless-steel cart positioned against the far wall. The wind is knocked out of me. Various laboratory tools and devices shoot into the air, and a din of noise echoes through the lab as the cart tumbles over on top of me. My eyes, blazing with fury, gaze up at him in amazement.

Stygius Cryptus just stands there, solemnly, watching me. "Forgive me," he says, presently, studying his own fist. "I do not readily approve of the use of my cybernetic strength protocols against humans. It is, in fact, a violation of my programming. However, you left me with little choice, Jax. I promise not to do it again."

I say nothing in response. I just lay there and let my head slowly fall to the floor as I wheeze for oxygen.

"Can you breathe?" he asks, mechanically.

I nod, though I'm really lying. My lungs are on fire, and I strain for breath, which is painfully slow in coming. My temples are pulsating with a powerful frenzy. I'm not sure which one he zapped, but both are resounding pain.

"Slowly, Jax," Cryptus says. "Breathe slowly. Your diaphragm has spasmed. Tension has seized it, and it has contracted. Take slow, deep breaths. Don't struggle. Let it happen naturally, and let your body recover. You should be yourself again in a few moments, perhaps quickly enough to forgive me for employing my superior design."

Superior design? I think to myself. *You can't even remember our conversation about the blue pen, you synthetic twit.*

But it doesn't matter. I need to breathe.

I let it go, and decide to do as he says, breathing naturally and slowly, telling myself I was going to even before Cryptus suggested it. The truth, however, is that it's hard to breathe normally through sobbing. And that's exactly what I do now: sob.

The android silently strolls over behind me and lifts the cart upright once more, righting it, then proceeds to gather the displaced equipment that pepper the floor around my prostrate form.

My diaphragm relaxes, just as he said it would. I take a deep, cleansing breath and wipe my eyes, streaking my face with the tears I had shed both in The Phoenix Experiment and in real life. I pull away from him and sit against the wall, my head bowed over my knees. I can't see Cryptus, but I hear him sit down on the far end of the room. He sighs, if you can call it that. We all know synthetics don't require air.

"Congratulations, Jax," he says quietly. "You *did* finally find them. I support that, and it is, of course, the very reason why we are here. However, I did what I did because you were clearly losing control."

I lift my head slowly, icily boring holes into him from across the room.

"As I mentioned, your reaction is not atypical for a first encounter with your parents," he says, and I realize that was word for word from what the robot had said before. "I assure you that others before you have exhibited the same type of emotional response upon re-encountering their loved ones."

"Which others?" I growl, quickly and angrily.

Cryptus frowns. "I am not permitted to disclose medical findings except with the subject of said findings. I am sure you understand that. But you are free to discourse your and others' experiences with your contemporaries as you see fit."

I just stare at him.

"You are well aware of our protocol here. The entire reason The Origin and The Zephyr exist is to prepare you for a stable return to Earth as a Speaker, and to equip you to deal with our adversaries effectively, without failing. Your overly emotional response compromised the integrity of your focus, as I'm sure you realized."

This is too much for me. Thankfully, I've regained my steady breathing by now. "You can't honestly expect us to *finally* reconnect with our parents and *not* be emotional, Cryptus. It's...," -here I try to employ a word that might resonate with him- "illogical!"

"As I have now stated twice, your reaction is not atypical for a first encounter with your parents," he replies emotionlessly. "But how you control that reaction needs to be typical. Your ability to master your emotions is the crux of whether or not you will successfully mature and develop as an effective Speaker against the banshees on Earth. That is why I needed to shock you out of your experiment once you reconnected with your parents. It happens with all of you. I've had to use this on every subject here. Please rest assured that will be the only time I use it on you. You are on your own to control your emotions from this point forward. Some subjects require," -here he pauses, ostensibly searching for the right word- "*motivation* in order to pull them out." I glance past him to his sinister and mysterious device docked over by the far wall.

I just glare at him. He is correct, of course, but that doesn't make it any better. It's worse, actually. As I just glare at him – feeling 4 years old and in trouble yet again – I think back to that episode with him forgetting the pen. Here he is lecturing me on effectiveness, yet he malfunctioned only a short time ago.

"Why didn't you remember the pen?" I ask him, point blank. "Tell me," I challenge him.

His head tilts and his eyes squint. "I'm sorry, Jax, I still don't understand the reference. Yet you continue to bring this up. Should I be concerned for your mental acuity and request a bio scan?"

I'm simply incredulous, and I can't hide it anymore.

I shake my head, and look up, overenunciating in my obvious disdain. "Phiria, play Reference Video 837.92.8A, outer Phoenix corridor vent aperture, on Phoenix Lab monitor 1, please." I only remember the number because of the five times that I was reminded it by Phiria in our morning summaries. For the five morning summaries we received following the incident, there was a glaring number reminding Anther and I to behave. That video reference number was on each summary.

A glowing blue circlet appears on the ceiling in response to my call. "Certainly, Ensign Hutson."

Cryptus turns his head over to the monitor as it lights up.

Two young boys emerge through the vent aperture, one of them sporting a giant blue splotch down their chest, the result of a leaking pen. Suddenly, a hulking figure blocks their path, and they cower.

Ensigns Hutson and Secto. What were you doing in the maintenance shaft?

Nothing, Mr. Cryptus. Sorry. We were just-

You are aware of Regulation 24B.9 which restricts all human passage to traversable areas only?

Yessir. We're sorry, Mr. Cryptus.

You should not be here. Spying on Ensign Filipath's Phoenix experiment? How deplorable. I shall have to report this to Helmsman Oculus and First Officer Mirabay post-haste. This area is strictly-

"I have seen enough," Cryptus says in a fatigued tone, and the monitor switches off.

"Certainly. Thank you, Stygius," Phiria says. She is the only one who calls him by his first name, I think.

"Jax," Cryptus says, rising. "I have but one question for you." He walks the entire way over to me, pausing in front of me. For a brief moment I think back to his fist, and wonder if he's now going to kick me into oblivion as I sit here. But my fears are allayed as he squats in front of me and inquires softly, "Do you trust me?"

I honestly don't know what to say. I'm shell-shocked from that punch, shell-shocked from finally finding my parents, shell-shocked from the whole ordeal. Deep down, I don't know if I trust Cryptus after the Zaris incident, and now especially after this one. All this time I've tried to reconnect with my parents, and now that these girls arrive, I finally do, in the midst of all of this swirling emotion?

But I'm better than him. Smarter. I can fool him. Time to 'overlook' the punch, and play it cool.

"Ye-yes," I stutter. I clear my throat and try again. "Yes, Cryptus, I trust you."

He nods, and I'm sure he sees right through me.

"Good. I want you to know that sometimes, in order to serve the greater good, I must challenge you. My entire occupation programming is predicated on challenge, improvement and bettering my shipmates, preparing them for their eventual return. If that requires me to bend the rules somewhat, to feign any behaviors incommensurate with synthetic operation, or to propel you into an unstable emotional state in order to gauge your recovery time, all in order to fulfill my programming, then I will do so, without your leave or the leave of Helmsman Oculus. I have been granted special medical allowances and provisions that facilitate my operation in this capacity. I trust that you know I do this for the greater good."

I tilt my head. "So, you remembered the pen all along, and were playing mind-games with me," I say. It isn't a question.

"Of course. I am an android, Jax. AnthroMeta Model K100 Series A. I always will be. It is impossible for me to forget anything. Even," he pauses, practically winking at me, "blue ink-filled pens. As I mentioned, my entire programming is intended to challenge, improve and better you."

Now I find that I'm suspicious of him that his memory was just jogged somehow by my playing the video through Phiria, and he did *not*, in fact, remember it all along. I also think he reads my thoughts. But I resign myself to try to trust him. For now.

"I have been, and evermore shall be, your humble servant here aboard The Origin and beyond. Please forgive me for assaulting you. I was simply acting out of self-preservation."

So was I, you cybernetic nitwit, I think.

Anther just stares at me, his mouth agape, and then he rushes at me and hugs me. If there's one thing that can be said about meatheads, they're also emotional. Maybe that's what fills all that meat: raw emotions.

"Congrats, dude, that's great!" he exclaims as he pulls away. "Seriously. That's great, bro. I'm happy for you."

Martos and Venthix are equally congratulatory, even though they're still on restriction from rec, and are bored out of their minds. They both come over and high-five me. The others are elsewhere aboard this vast ship, doing assigned tasks, meeting with Oculus, guiding the girls' chiefs Ashira Sarristo and Maridie Onyx and familiarizing them with The Origin, even though they've already been here for a few days. But, given The Rubris' estimated time of arrival, they're going to be here for a while.

"Thanks, guys," I say. We fist bump.

"Took ya long enough," Venthix fires my way, sitting down across from me. I roll my eyes. "No, seriously! I'm happy for you! Now Garris can really suck it. Ha!"

I laugh. Garris still hasn't found his parents, and I wonder why that hasn't bonded us together all this time, at the very least providing us a common bond to mourn over. But he's an oaf, and always will be. Nonetheless, I find myself silently wishing him well in the aftermath of Anther's comment.

"Garris should find his someday. It was… surreal. But Cryptus pulled the plug practically right after I found them," I end mournfully. "It really pissed me off."

"Oh yeah, he did that to me, too," Venthix agrees, slouching. "Pissed me off royally too."

"Me too," chimes in Martos. His left cheek still sports a purple welt from Venthix's right hook. "He does that to everyone."

I look at Anther in amazement. He just nods. His expression says the same happened to him.

I squint my eyes. "He does?"

Anther nods swiftly. "Yeah, dude. Of course he does." He glances over at the other two like this is the most outlandish thing he's heard all day. "Why wouldn't he? We freak out, right? It's our *parents*, man. Of course we're gonna become blubbering wrecks. They can't have us all softies when we go back down. That defeats the purpose of our whole stay here. Duh," he ends, with another side-eyed smile at the others like I'm an idiot.

"I didn't know that."

All of them just nod.

"Don't let it get you down, though, man. You should celebrate! The fact that you got to them? Means there's hope," Venthix says. "Good job, dude. You focused enough to do it. That's the beginning."

I'm heartened by this. "Okay. Okay. That makes sense. Thanks, Venthix," I say. My heart is lifted after all that has transpired. "I'm just glad that he only had to do the zapper thing on me once. He said that would be the only time. I guess I should be relieved." I flick my eyebrows up and sigh gratefully, ending with a nervous chuckle.

The others just stare at me, not connecting the dots. I pan my gaze around the room. Their expression is identical between all of them, and I'm confused. "What?" I ask them. "The zapper? He said he used that on all of you too."

Anther frowns, shaking his head and looking at the other guys. "Cryptus never had to use anything like that on me," he says, staring at the others for validation. They all shake their heads. *Nope*, both of them concur.

I'm flummoxed. And now I'm pissed again.

In all of this, I realize two stark, naked truths:

One, Cryptus lied to me.

And two, I do *not* trust him. I don't know that I ever really did.

I just grit my teeth in frustration.

My irritation is deep down in my soul, and I'm grimacing hard.

6: The Emotions

I see her, clearly, and my heart leaps.

There's Alaris. Fresh off the connection with my parents, and the subsequent revelation that Cryptus lied to me, I decide I need some fresh air and go for a walk.

Fresh air, I think, as I head toward the observation deck. *Yeah, right.* The carbon dioxide on this ship is purified and recycled, constantly ionized and recirculated for us to exist here, indefinitely. The

Origin is solar-powered, our air is endless, and as long as we have enough revolting *BioPrime* to sustain us, we'll live, grow old and die. If we don't choke on our own vomit from the disgusting food goo first, that is.

I round a corner, and there she is.

I haven't seen her in a few days, but I decide right away that this is just the emotional uplift I need on the coattails of such startling developments.

She's just lingering there: quietly, coldly, her arms crossed, her eyes glued on some distant star in the thick galaxy beyond her diminutive frame. She is utterly beautiful in her silent enamor, and her fixation prevents her from hearing me. My feet slow as I behold her.

> *Beyond the void, adrift by star,*
> *The black of cold doth silence mar*
> *For lives forlorn*
> *with hope unborn*
> *Spin irretrievably afar*
>
> *And time: a cruel and merciless haunt*
> *To stalk the soul consumed by want*
> *The young grow old,*
> *and hearts turn cold*
> *Yet longing holds, now frail and gaunt*

I don't want to startle her, so I figure now would be a good time to clear my throat. I do so.

She startles.

Nice goin,' Jax. Smooth.

"Hey, Alaris," I say, sheepishly, putting my hands up. "Sorry, I didn't mean to scare you." I offer a meek smile.

Her cold visage instantly transforms into warmth as she regards me. "Hey. Nice to see you again. Jax, right?" Her pale skin seems awash in color now as she rotates her body to face me.

"Yeah," I say nervously as I draw near. "We haven't met yet. I-I saw you when you came off the Avalon, but," I stammer, "yeah. Been a few days. What's your last name again? Sorry, I can't remember."

"Rederium."

"That's right. I'm Jax-"

"Hutson," she finishes for me. "I know."

I smile. "Rederium, huh? Your hair color is in your last name."

"Yep," she says with a slight eye roll. "Imagine that."

I perceive that I've slipped up somehow. Maybe she's sensitive about her hair color, or just her hair itself. I don't know how she could be; it's one of her most stunning features. I gather myself. *Time to change the subject, Jax.* "Uh, h-how are you liking The Origin so far? Are you guys all comfortable and settled in now?"

She musters a nod and looks around briefly, surveying our ship, identical to her own which perished. "It's alright. Almost the same, right? I mean, it's *all* the same. Everything is the same out here, day after day."

She takes on a dour tone with that last comment, and I can tell she's suffering from the same doldrums as most all of us are, or at least have at one point or another. She stares out at the stars again, wistfully.

I attempt a little light humor as I draw even nearer to her. "Oh, it's not so bad," I say. "I mean, you get tired of strawberry *BioPrime*, you can always try lemon *BioPrime*. And if that gets old, you get to switch to blueberry *BioPrime*. Or vanilla *BioPrime*. And then there's everybody's favorite, green apple *BioPrime*. So, ya know. Variety."

By now Alaris is giggling, and our mutual disdain for our revolting slop binds us together as two lost sojourners desperate for a little lighthearted respite. "You're so right. What I wouldn't give for a little-"

"Steak?" I interrupt, smiling.

Her face whips back over to mine, only a few seductive inches away. "Yes! Steak! How did you know?"

I shake my head. "I know things about people. You just have that face that says, 'I'd like a steak, please.'"

"Oh, do I?" She giggles again. I'm receiving full marks for handsomeness, charm, *and* humor here. Briefly I envision all the other guys, from Anther, to Garris, to Martos, to Venthix, even to Ranshay and little Dravin, all of them, eating crow – while Alaris and I feast on steak – and turning away in defeat.

"Yeah. Well, I wouldn't get your hopes up. Never had one here either, and I'm still wondering what it tastes like. Omnias wants lobster, apparently. One of these days I think we're gonna go over the edge, steal the Avalon, and head down to Earth to pig out, banshees be damned."

"Banshees be damned," she concurs with a grin, and then she sizes me up. "You're kinda cute, you know that?"

I smile wholeheartedly at this direct-approach affirmation, and I feel the heat in my face. *She thinks I'm cute.* "Thanks. You're not too bad, yourself."

"I wanted to reach out to you earlier, but one of the guys told me that you were interested in someone else. Garris? I think that's his name."

I shake my head definitively. "Garris is not my friend. He's a slab of meat with legs. He knows nothing," I dismiss.

Alaris chuckles. "Ha! That's funny. Slab of meat. *Now* who has steak on the brain?"

I take her point instantly. "Touché," I shrug with a grin. "How have you liked your sessions here so far? Is it weird doing them with Cryptus instead of your own synthetic?"

She shakes her head and props herself up against the glass pane, framed by stars. A pale light is about her, and my heart swoons at the sight. Poetry courses through me. She is gorgeous in every way.

"Not really. They all talk the same anyway, right? I hear yours is British."

"Only because he wants to be. What's yours?"

"Talicus thinks she's Asian. Has the whole accent down. She's alright. She switched a few years ago from Russian, and Jamaican before that. I liked Jamaican better." She nervously fidgets with her hair. "What about you? I heard something went haywire with Zaris the other day or something. Omnias told us. Freaky."

I shrug and quasi-roll my eyes. "Cryptus. Yeah, he's a strange bird. I dunno. He's good at what he does, but they're all just creepy. All of 'em. I don't trust them," I finish, waving the conversation away.

I don't want to talk with Alaris about androids. I want to talk with Alaris about Alaris. "How many experiments have you done? Have you ever…?"

She nods before I finish my question. "Found my parents? Yep. Finally. Took me a while," she huffs with a noisome exhale.

"Me too."

"Yeah?"

"Yeah," I agree. "I actually only just found mine today."

She gasps.

"*Today?*" she asks, astonished. "Seriously? As in, like, a few hours ago. Wow. That's crazy! Well, I'm really glad for you. Sorry it took so long! How many sessions have you done?"

"Innumerable. I'm over 1500 somewhere."

"Same," she says. "How long have you been on The Origin?"

"Five years now."

"Wow, same here too. Did you lose your parents a while before you came here, or-?"

I nod, quickly. "A few months prior. Took me a while to get a shuttle."

She studies me for a moment. "It's so weird, isn't it? Us being kept apart on opposite sides of the planet for so long. It's not like we're gonna be all crazy and unfocused just because we're together. Your loss binds you to your guy friends, our loss binds us to our girlfriends. Same difference, right?"

"I think so," I concur. "But, you know,' we're steak-craving wild and uncontrollable boys with hormones, right? At least, that's how Oculus sees us."

She shrugs. "Oh well. He's wrong," she states emphatically, regarding me proudly. "At least about *one* of them. Maybe not so much about the meat slab guy, but you?" She looks me over, pretending to size me up. "I think you're okay."

"A minute ago, I was cute, and now I'm just 'okay'? Fine. I get it. Tough downgrade, though," I pout, feigning offense.

"Stop it, goofball," she says, playfully gripping my bicep, and I spastically find myself flexing. I'm not Orin, but I hope she notices. "Hey, when do you do rec time?"

"Depends on whenever I'm done with Cryptus and daily duties. Usually 1500 hours if I have a morning session, or 2000 hours if it's an afternoon one. You guys can join us for rec? Isn't that too close to *fraternization* for our chiefs' tastes?"

"I don't think so, silly. We just have to ask for permission each time. I don't know that anyone has asked yet. I'll probably have more luck if I ask Sarristo or Onyx for us to double-date."

"Double date?" I ask.

"Yeah, if we go with Mr. Meat Slab and one of the girls that he fancies. Or someone you recommend."

I'm up for a challenge, so my mind instantly goes to Anther. "I can think of someone good. Are you friends with Omnias?"

"Yeah! I don't really know her all that well, doesn't she like that one guy, Anter, Ather…?"

"*Anther*," I correct her, laughing that no one seems to get either of his names correctly. "Ant's a decent chap. Yeah, that would be fun. How can you find me and let me know you got permission? I had a morning session and I was going to go this afternoon, but now it looks more like it'll be tonight. So, the 2000 hours rec slot."

"I'll let Phiria know to get you a message," she says, and then she pauses, staring at my lips.

"Cool." I notice her pause, and I feel my eyebrows eventually raise in curiosity. "Was there something else?"

"No. Well, yes, actually. Please don't think me forward, but, have you ever been kissed?"

My eyebrows again. "Uh, I don't think so, I-"

Before I know it, she leans in to me and kisses me passionately. The warmth of her mouth envelops mine, and senses I didn't even know I had awoke to the promise of newness. Her eyes are closed, and then I realize I should close mine as well. It's quick, it's brief, it's unexpected, and it's utterly amazing. I can taste some kind of lip balm, some fruit flavor I can't readily identify. Alaris slowly pulls away, and I feel like biting her lips just to keep them in mine.

I feel a heatwave pass through me as I reflexively laugh with unbridled joy. "That – was – cool. And actually, now that I think about it, *have* been kissed," I joke, meaning her. "Thanks, Alaris."

She giggles. "No. Thank *you*, Jax," she says through a gleeful smile, and her knees appear to buckle briefly as she slips past me, her eyes fluttering.

"K. Yeah. Uh, I mean, you're welcome. I, uh-" I try, stammering, "I should be getting back too. Gotta do… stuff. You know." I fidget with my hair. My shirt. My pants. My foot stretches out and absentmindedly scruffs at something on the ground while my arms do things outside of my control. I've gone to pieces somehow in the heat of this sensory overload.

"Yeah," I finish lamely.

She stops walking and turns around, eyeing me quizzically. "You know," she starts, "I don't think it was an accident that we had… *the accident*. Fate has brought us together, Jax. You and me."

I smile, agreeing. "I believe it," I say.

She beams back at me. "I'll have Phiria let you know. See ya, Jax."

"See ya. Alaris," I say, in two distinct sentences, feebly and utterly consumed by feeling.

> *For longing lingereth strong and fast*
> *And pleadeth not to far outlast*
> > *The doldrum's drudge,*
> > *the grasping sludge*
> *Restoring pulse to hearts that passed*

With everything in me, I can't wait for rec time tonight. *I'm a wild dog, and I'm okay with it,* I think.

Restoring pulse to hearts that passed.

I kissed her, tenderly, and my heart leapt.

7: The Surprise

Phiria sends the message. I get to meet Alaris.

With that, I change into my athletic garb and carry a small duffle bag with me for a change of clothes afterward.

Rec hall is the largest area on The Origin. It's got a full basketball court, swimming pool, hot tub, tabletop games, ping-pong, air hockey, couches, relaxation pods, neural beds to unwind in, and so much more. Martos and Venthix really are missing out. Hell, *anyone* who doesn't get rec misses out. I never see Oculus or Mirabay in here, so I don't know if they're missing out or not. Maybe they just use it when the rest of us are asleep or something. But it's the thing we boys look forward to most on this ship every day.

With the obvious exception, now, of seeing girls, that is.

On the way to rec, I overtake the girls' synthetic, Baryonnis Talicus. She greets me cordially and then gets straight to the point: she is there to ensure there is no funny business, though I can't imagine what she thinks that means, given what I've seen her contemporary do. Her Asian accent is weird.

I watch her, curiously, as she walks beside me with a patronizing smile, a presence both unwanted and unneeded. *I'm not a child,* I think to myself. I know how to behave, and I don't need a robot – of the same model series as Cryptus – telling me what to and what not to do. I have a leg up on both of them. I know now to lie, I know not to play with people's emotions, and I know how to be human. All things that Cryptus – and presumably, Talicus – *don't* know.

"I'm actually late," she says. "Several of your contemporaries are already there, as are the females."

Females? *So weird. So formal,* this male thinks to himself.

She accompanies me on an awkward stroll through our corridors, all the way to the rec hall. She even holds the door open for me, though I didn't ask. I'm beginning to really tire of these synthetics. No wonder all this time we only had a single android on board. One is too much; two is overkill. We already have Phiria, and I daresay we all now know how to hook each other up for the Phoenix Experiments and do them ourselves. Phiria could walk us through it remotely if she or we wanted her to, instead of having these intimidating, patronizing synthetics haunting our every step.

And – bonus – she couldn't zap us out with that stupid electronic device.

I walk in, and there's Alaris. My eyes drink in her beauty, *and* the beauty of her form, as she is sporting high shorts and a shirt that cuts off high enough to provide me with ample view of her midriff. She is *all* legs. I truly don't know what to say. I cast a quick glance at Talicus to see if she is giving Alaris a disapproving glare, but I see no such sign.

Briefly, I wonder what exactly constitutes 'funny business' in a synthetic's mind. But I don't have more time to wonder.

"Jax!" Alaris shouts, and heads my way. "*There* you are. I was wondering when you were going to get here." A few other girls walk over with her my way.   When they reach me, they assertively turn to Talicus. Alaris says, "Thank you, Talicus, that will be all."

The synthetic nods and then retreats to a far wall to observe, and presumably, monitor and record any perceived misbehavior to their chiefs. Makes me want to intentionally misbehave.

But I raise my eyebrows. I'm genuinely impressed. I don't know that I've ever 'dismissed' Cryptus, but I resolve to try that sometime soon. My estimation of Alaris just elevates.

Looking around quickly, I can see Orin is here; he's down swimming with Miritia. They're both scantily clad. The thought crosses my mind that Talicus should be minding *that* and not us more appropriately-clad youths down here who aren't showing so much skin. That's when I spot Anther amongst the girls. He now strolls up beside Omnias to greet me. Little Ranshay and Dravin are playing ping-pong off by themselves, girl-less and naïve as can be. Anther gives me a typical 'sup' nod and stands by my side. I tone down the force, but I give him a nice play-slug in the shoulder again. He smiles.

"I see you ladies have met Anther," I say. "Hopefully he hasn't terrorized you too much?" They giggle and nod amongst themselves.

That's when I spot little Zaris behind them, and regret the 'terror' question. She was concealed behind Skarbé, Donetis, and Ghirisha. I applaud myself for remembering their names. She looks fine now.

Omnias is off to the side, twirling one of her pigtails and watching Anther approvingly, but I wonder, in seeing her like that, if she's completely forgotten what we saw in the lab together that day.

"Something wrong, Jax?" Alaris asks me.

"Hmm?" I ask, jerking back. "Oh! Nothing. Let's do this! What are you guys wanting to do first?"

The girls glance at each other quickly with a knowing expression, and before I know it, a ball comes out of nowhere and bops me in the face as the girls – and Anther – scatter, giggling. I rub my forehead and collect myself briefly, scooping up the ball and searching for my target.

Bean The Beaner it is. Haven't played this in a while. It's a great, fun game that involves nothing more than hurling a ball at someone's head as hard as you can, and if they swoon, you get a point. If they topple, you get three points. We've played it plenty of times on The Origin. The girls must have had similar rec layouts and programs. It hasn't yet drawn blood and allows us to pummel things: an ingenious and convenient way of letting off steam when we don't find our parents. Garris plays it often.

I pursue them. Well, mostly I pursue Omnias since I'm pretty sure she was the one who threw it. My first throw goes awry. Girls are scattering everywhere. Anther is running with Omnias. He sees my shot miss her, and he turns to retrieve it but it bounces against the wall and heads back my way. We're about equidistant from the ball. I see him start to pick up speed, and he flashes me a devilish grin suggesting he'll beat me to it. But he forgets that I'm the skinny, spry one. I make it to the ball first, diving into it and clutching it to myself as he topples into me with a clumsy thud. We both laugh, and he gets up, because now he's a target. It doesn't matter who the target is in *Bean the Beaner*: everyone counts. I could hurl it at Baryonnis Talicus and score an easy three points. But I don't. The thought flashes through my head that if Cryptus were here, I'd for sure hurl it at him. Over and over.

Anther has had enough time to put distance between us. He's howling with laughter at our collision, rubbing his shoulder while he races away, back toward Omnias. He points her around a corner and they hide. I'm back on my feet and in pursuit of the other girls. I locate my target.

She's a lithe red-head, and she's my age. She's wearing high shorts, and those legs draw me in as she runs. That beautiful midriff calls to me as I close the gap between us. The other girls flee from this wild dog, as I chase after Alaris and prepare to bean her with all the savage force of a dandelion. They instantly realize that they were never my target, and they slow their pace. They know who I only have eyes for.

Alaris dashes over to the air hockey tables and hides behind them. I'm on her in no time. I duck down. There she is, on the other side. She giggles, raising up above the table in a stutter-step. But there I am, my hand upraised.

Dare I hurl this ball at her at such close range? She's laughing now, but I don't want to bean this beaner. Not this one.

Alaris sticks her tongue out at me playfully, and that thought is quickly extinguished. Then she's back underneath the table once more.

Now's my chance!

I start to make my way around. Alaris is aware of me. She shrieks and begins to take off. I give chase.

Wild dog in pursuit.

She's no match for my spry legs. But speaking of legs – *oh those legs* – I watch them jostle up and down in front of me as she tries to escape. I have her. My sights lock on her form, and she's all mine. I raise my arm. I can bean her in the back and not feel so bad.

Before I'm even aware of it, tiny feet have sped up behind me, noiselessly, and a small arm knocks my own downward as I go into my wind up and prepare to hurl the small rubber ball at my new love interest. The projectile goes askew, bouncing clumsily off the side wall as I whip around to my right in amazement.

An angry voice rails at me, and I stop dead in my tracks. "Stop that! Leave her alone, Jax Hutson!" the high-pitched voice cries. It's Zaris, and her eyes are red and wild with heat. I don't know her, but I recognize offense when I see it. She's panting from running so flat-out to catch up with me, and as she scowls at me, she does so under her eyebrows. I too, am panting, just watching her in amazement.

"You're an evil, evil boy, Jax Hutson!" she rails at me, pointing an accusatory finger at me, two inches from my face. She doesn't back off, and she's breathing hard. "Evil!"

Talicus leaves her post on the wall and instantly scurries over to Zaris, who by now begins to burst into tears as we standoff. I watch as the girls' synthetic rushes over to her, embraces her, wraps a fake meaty arm around her and strides off with her. The android gives me a quick look of consolation as if to assure me I haven't done anything wrong, and then she's walking off with the young girl, leaving me standing there, catching my breath.

I have no idea what I've done.

And then, the cold truth hits me: Zaris is clearly still traumatized from her Phoenix session.

Presently, I become dimly aware of someone suddenly standing to my left. I turn to see Alaris by my side, and she's panting too. Her skin glistens. "Hey, don't worry about it," she says. "She gets a little overreactive from time to time. She can be protective of us."

My eyebrows flick up in amazement. I start to say something, but then I catch Omnias staring at me with a worried expression. She says nothing, but quickly retreats and follows Zaris and Talicus out of the rec hall. My mind flashes back once more to the lab. And Cryptus. And the device.

"Has she always been like that, or just for the past few days?" I ask between breaths.

Alaris stares at me, confused.

Anther walks up to us. It's obvious he's hiding something. I can see it in his eyes. He's remembering our conversation from four days ago, and it's clear he and Omnias have talked about it as well. After all, she was there with me. She saw the whole thing too.

"Jax, don't," he says to me under his breath.

I crinkle my nose at him, confused. "Don't what?? I just-"

"Dude! Don't!" he interrupts me, placing a hand on my chest suddenly. "Let it go!"

I look at Alaris, dumbfounded.

"Uh, we gotta go, okay? Somebody ate too much *BioPrime* and needs a little reeducation," Anther says to her. "Sorry."

Alaris watches me, equally dumbfounded. "Sure, it's fine. I mean – yeah, it's f-fine," she finishes in a stutter.

I glance around at the other girls, and they're all apparently as shell-shocked as I am. Orin and Miritia are sitting at the edge of the pool, dangling their feet in the water, but they've both craned their backs to us, wondering what all the hubbub was about. For myself, I have no idea, and it's making me mad.

Anther grabs me by the arm. "Come on."

He starts off with me toward the door, but I wrench myself free of his grasp. "I'm capable of walking by myself, thanks," I say to him firmly, in no mood to be downplayed in front of Alaris – or *anyone,* for that matter. "Let's go," I command him.

I look back at Alaris one final time, and she's downcast. What started out as a fun first date has obviously gone south in a hurry, all because of some mysterious outburst that I'm about to learn much more about from Anther, apparently.

"See ya soon," I assure her, and she nods quickly. "Chow time?" I ask.

"Yeah. Sure," she says, but then she glances nervously at the other girls.

I haven't a clue what all of this bizarre affair is about, but I sure hope to find out soon. My gut says that whatever Cryptus allowed – or did – in Zaris' Phoenix Experiment left a lasting mark on her psyche. I am determined to find out what that was.

> *All is never what it seems,*
> *Mystery eateth at the seams*
> > *Veneers lie deep;*
> > *pretense a keep*
> *To confound in daze and blinding gleam…*
>
> *But conscience sayeth trust thy guess*
> *Lest hunch fall prey to deep duress*
> > *The truth is oft*
> > *not far aloft*
> *But within reach, despite the mess…*

Hearing the whispers inside my brain, I walk out of there with Anther, our voices hushed.

I am now sitting in the library with Anther and Omnias. Zaris is back in her quarters with Talicus. Alaris and the rest of them are, presumably, still up in rec. It seems the only youths who *didn't* see it are Venthix and Martos, understandably.

Ignorance is bliss.

Towering rows of books cascade around us: an abundance of literature from so many centuries of a planet unfortunately long bereft of an abundance of readers.

"I want to talk with Oculus," I say, defiantly. "And Mirabay."

"Dude, don't go up against Cryptus, man," Anther warns me. "You don't want him on your bad side. Don't do it, Jax."

"What does that mean? Why? He might be doing something to them. To *us!* How do we know he hasn't been doing something all along?" I counter.

Omnias watches us ping-pong back and forth.

"Jax, this is all based off of *one* circumstance. You're not thinking clearly! The girls got here and messed with our emotions – no offense, Omni," he says to her and then turns back to me, "and you're just a giddy kid who's not thinking clearly right now."

"Fine. I'm willing to take that chance, though. Why *shouldn't* I go to our helmsman if I think something is up? I've never experienced that in my Phoenix Experiments. Have you?"

"No, but-"

"See? Have *you*, Omnias?"

She quietly shakes her head. "I've never seen anything like that. And I've watched Zaris here and there. And others. And they've watched me. When we first started, we would watch each other because it was new. Unpredictable. We wanted to make sure we were okay. We were just looking out for each other," she says.

"I hear you! And that's all I want to do here, Ant. I barely know Zaris, but I'm looking out for her too. Cryptus has been doing and saying strange things for the past week. You didn't see what Omnias and I saw, man. You didn't see the third chair. You *weren't* there. It was evil, man."

Anther sighs and shrugs his shoulders. He crosses his arms and turns away from me. "Come on," he argues. "Evil, Jax? Really *Evil*?" he asks, turning back to me, with a look of utter incredulity denting his face. "Apparently, Zaris thinks *you're* evil. She's just a little girl, man!"

I think back to what Zaris said, her finger in my face. Anther does have a point. I certainly don't *feel* evil. "Anther, come on, bro. You've known me for a long time. Have I changed?"

He doesn't answer.

"Seriously! Have I changed at all?"

He quietly shakes his head. "No."

I turn to Omnias. "Has Zaris changed? I'm not saying she's evil, Omnias. I'm not saying that at all. But is she different since she's been aboard The Origin and especially since that Phoenix session?"

Omnias thinks to herself for a moment, then quietly nods, and crosses her own arms, lost in thought. Anther sat down on a library bench in a huff.

"Okay, then," I say, feeling I've scored a point. "I'm the same. Zaris isn't. Something happened to her. That something was the Phoenix Experiment with Cryptus. Oculus needs to know. He said it himself before they even came on board: *They must be kept safe, by all of us,* he said. He needs to know if even one of them is not being kept safe, Anther. Right?" I hold my arms out, awaiting his reply. Omnias shifts as she stands, her eyes darting between the two of us. She has to know I was right, at least. Now it's just about convincing my meathead friend of the same.

Anther finally relents. "Fine," he mumbles under his breath. "Talk to Oculus. But Jax," he says, looking up at me under his brows with a piercing stare, "remember I warned you about going up against Cryptus."

I listen to him, but I'm not ready to nod or receive his warning. It doesn't hold much weight, at least for the moment. Sure, Cryptus can be intimidating, but if I've warned Oculus and Mirabay about him, then I've got our helmsman and First Officer on my side.

> *Onus and burden, duty and charge*
> *Summon the virtuous, small to large*
> *The truth must out,*
> *Through scandalous doubt*
> *lest miscreants their evil ways recharge*
>
> *So don boldness readily, push forward steadily*

> *And keep thy countenance as thou move headily*
> *Know thy course just,*
> *proceed as thou must*
> *'til truth is declared, winning succor incredibly*

Message received. I head off to meet with Oculus.

8: The Confrontation

I look him squarely in the eye, standing my ground.

"Helmsman Oculus, sir, I'm telling the truth. I've never seen anything like that before. Omnias saw it too," I declare, firmly.

"Omnias was there with you in the foyer?" he asks me, clearly annoyed by this news. Mirabay glances once at him, and then back at me.

"Yessir. She will attest to the same thing."

Oculus just studies me for a moment, his arms crossed, his fist to his chin, scowling. His eyes drop to the floor, lost in thought for a moment.

"Jax, Cryptus informed me that you recently made contact with your parents this morning during your Phoenix Experiment, is that correct?"

"Yes, sir," I say, feeling a well of emotion at the memory of it.

"He reports that this was the first time. How are you feeling now?"

"I'm… exhilarated, sir. It was surreal, and wonderful, and unexpected all at onc-" I reply, but then I stop, catching the meaning of his question. It's a snare, and I recognize it instantly. "Wait. You're not just casually asking me about that. You're doubting my emotional state because of my finally making contact with my parents in my session, wondering now if I'm not thinking clearly because I'm… overwhelmed or something?" I stare at him under my brow, feeling hot. Mirabay watches me accusingly. Oculus mirrors him.

But then, the helmsman can't contain himself, and he erupts into spontaneous laughter, punctuating his own dreariness. "Gotta say, Jax, you're a pistol. Sharp as a tack and call a spade a spade."

"Sir," I feel the need to clarify, "I'm *fine*. This incident happened four days ago. My contact with my parents was this morning. Again, Omnias can corroborate all of this, I assure you. This incident predates whatever emotional state I might even be in given my recent contact. Surely you can see that Cryptus is up to something."

The helmsman finally takes a deep breath. "Fair enough. However, if this was so important, why didn't you come to me earlier? Couldn't it be that you're a bit frazzled and emotional *now* given your breakthrough with your parents? Cryptus also informed me he had to pull you out of your session prematurely with a bit of a… *jolt.*" Now he's staring at me with his tongue halfway out his mouth, his eyebrows up, his head cocked downward at me. An expression of distrust is written all over him. "So, frankly, this sounds a bit like revenge." He looks to Mirabay for approval. The First Officer nods.

"Sir, that's not fair. That's not even *close* to the truth. Him pulling me out had nothing to do with my coming to you. Zaris' session, and, furthermore, her behavior today, reinforces my suspicion that Cryptus did something to her. He might be doing it to others as well. Before the crew of the Zephyr boarded our ship, you made it clear to all of us that you wanted us to keep them safe. All of us. Those were your words, Helmsman, meaning no disrespect. And none intended to you either, Mr. Mirabay."

Both study me for what seems like an interminable amount of time. I wait.

"And just what do you think he might have done to that young girl in her session, anyway, Jax? You think he scared her in her subconscious? Or he's doing something else untoward?"

I slowly shake my head. "Sir, I don't know. But you can have Omnias in here to corroborate my story. Or I'd even suggest bringing in Zaris and asking her directly. It was frightening, sir. Zaris – wasn't herself. At all. And then the third chair in the chamber had a dim shape in it. Almost like he had-" I stop, thinking back.

Oculus doesn't wait. "Had what?" he pries.

I take a deep breath. "I don't know, sir. It was like Cryptus was trying to bring an entity through the Phoenix connection. Bring it back *with* Zaris. Or… *through* her, even. It didn't look like human."

Oculus just continues to study me, incredulous.

Know thy course just,
proceed as thou must
'til truth is declared, winning succor incredibly

He is obviously conflicted, but there's a tired resolve in his eyes that tells me he wants to put this to bed quickly. I predict that will win over, and he'll easily dismiss this – and me – summarily.

But he surprises me anyway.

"Alright, Jax," Oculus says. "I'll have Cryptus in here and have a little chat. Are you comfortable being in our presence while he is presented with your assertions?"

I slowly nod, though I'd honestly prefer to stay as far away from Cryptus as possible. I have another session in two days… not tomorrow, but the following day, and I'm not looking forward to it. Depending on how this 'little chat' goes, I'll be looking forward to that session even less. I briefly consider overdosing on *BioPrime* instead, and save us all the trouble of any further conflagrations. But Alaris would be forlorn…

"Alright," he says. "Chow time is in 94 minutes. I'll summon him right away. He shouldn't be in session at the moment," -here he glances at his watch and then mirrors it at a chronograph on the wall- "so he should be free. Have a seat."

I comply, retreating to a chair against the entrance wall. Mirabay does the same, sitting perpendicular to me, closer to Oculus' desk.

My helmsman retreats behind his console and taps a key on his array. A short klaxon sounds throughout the ship, reverberating down the corridors behind us. "Stygius Cryptus, Stygius Cryptus, Helmsman Oculus. Please report to the Bridge."

He releases the button and slowly sits down behind his desk. We all sit in awkward silence. I can hear my heartbeat.

"I can't imagine what you think he might be doing to her in there. But we'll soon know, won't we?" Oculus casts a doubtful glance over at Mirabay, and the First Officer flicks his eyebrows up and then turns to watch me. He has a smirk on his face, and I want to slap it off of him.

I suddenly get cold feet, and I wish I wasn't here in his office.

I wish I hadn't seen anything with Omnias.

I wish I had never had a session on the coattails of Zaris,' nor that I had been there.

I even find myself wishing that the girls had never come here. A lot has changed since they've been here, and I don't know what to make of it. But no girls equals no Alaris, and I find that very notion utterly rejectable.

I wonder where Alaris is. I wonder what she's thinking. I wonder what the next kiss will feel like… or if there will even be one.

I truly want there to be one.

"Stygius, come in," Oculus greets him, noticing his presence but not looking up at him. He is occupied with observing reports and data from the bridge console. "Thank you for coming," he says, tiredly.

The synthetic walks in, a dry look on his face. "Helmsman Oculus," he acknowledges, and then he takes stock of the bridge and sees me sitting there. He appears unfazed. "Hello, Jax. First Officer Mirabay," he greets us as well, perhaps not yet sensing what's about to happen.

Stygius is calculating, however, I tell myself. He knows we're not seeing eye to eye. My chest reverberates faintly in memory of that reflexive punch he doled out. My mind resonates with anger at his pulling me out of my Phoenix experiment. My skin tingles with the bristling suspicion I have had since he lied to me.

Cryptus sits down between Mirabay and I. The synthetic slowly glances over at me, his eyes cold. He musters up a strange and discomfiting smile, and a strange pang of fear runs through me. Anther's words resound in my head.

Dude, don't go up against Cryptus, man. You don't want him on your bad side.

I briefly wonder what Cryptus could do to me in a Phoenix Experiment. I have no idea what he's capable of doing to me in my subconscious, and for a moment I wish I had spoken to Zaris more before she left, prying out of her the details of what she experienced in her own session with him.

The helmsman leans back in his chair, pulling away from his console and regarding all of us slowly.

"How is everything going on your end, Cryptus?"

The android straightens up. "Oh, fine, sir. All is well."

"We've had a little bit of added excitement around here lately, haven't we?" Oculus asks.

"You could say that, Helmsman. But I think everyone is responding and behaving appropriately, each according to their own stature and abilities."

"How do you mean?"

"Well, putting it delicately, sir, these hormone-filled children and adolescents – present company *included* of course with Ensign Hutson here – seem to be faring well in the presence of the opposite sex with all of the increased stimulation their presence provides. It's been a study in temperance."

"I see."

"They've been reasonably self-controlled, Helmsman Oculus. My colleague Baryonnis Talicus feels the same. Short of a recent outburst by one of their younger females, the girls have been well-behaved. And, notwithstanding Ensign Hutson's assaulting me today following the successful Phoenix Experiment he had-"

"Assaulted you?" Oculus interrupts, squinting at him. His eyes dart over to me. "Clarify. What is the meaning of this, Jax?"

This infuriates me, and I roll my eyes. Oculus is no doubt mad at this one-sided appraisal *and* the fact that I've not reported it to him. I sigh, taken at unawares by Cryptus' subtle yet tattletale-like report.

"Oculus, it wasn't an *assault,*" I say, quickly. "I was angry, yes. All this time I've sought to reconnect with my parents, and I only just did today. I was angry that he jerked me out of it," -here I flashed my eyes over at him icily- "but in no way did I assault him. I was grasping him like so," I say, demonstrating how I held his lapels, "but I was not violent in any way." I sigh in defeat as I glance at Oculus "*Yes*, I was shaking and screaming at him. But that didn't give him any reason to punch me hard in the chest." I enunciate these last words, staring accusingly at him.

My emphasis isn't lost on Oculus.

"You punched him in the chest?" Oculus asks the synthetic.

"So hard I flew backward and knocked over a medical tray," I quickly add.

Oculus' eyes flicker back to me, and then they returns to Cryptus. "Why did you do that? Isn't violence against humans strictly forbidden by AnthroMeta protocol and programming?"

"Forgive me, Helmsman," Cryptus says quietly. "Indeed it is. I was acting in self-defense, and I had warned Ensign Hutson – twice – to release me. He did not. I feared for my own safety."

"A grown adult android feared for his safety from a 14-year-old boy half his size?"

Cryptus is silent for a moment. "I take your point, Helmsman. I was, however, concerned. Self-preservation is our overriding protocol, just as it is for humans. Ensign Hutson was understandably upset, and as I had tried to communicate to him, his response was not atypical from the other youths aboard The Origin when they have encountered their own parents. Logic and reason become suspended in the emotional overwhelm that seizes them following such a heartfelt reunion. Jax was certainly no different in this regard, and his emotional outburst followed suit."

Oculus is silent. His eyes dart over to Mirabay's for a moment as he, presumably, strives to weigh the situation and judge justly. He sighs.

Mirabay watches him, rubbing his chin.

I don't look at Cryptus, but I can feel the heat of his stare upon me.

"Cryptus," Oculus continues, "Jax feels that you are perhaps operating inauthentically, and that you may be abusing your position as Phoenix conductor. It's clear to me that you assaulted Jax, not vice versa."

I feel a swell of vindication course through me. Maybe Cryptus is going to get it now.

"And now we must deal with this as well," Oculus states clearly. "Look at me, please. I, Helmsman Fulsar Oculus, invoke AnthroMeta Primary Protocol 11A and order you to tell me the truth and nothing but. What happened – precisely – during Ensign Sharibian's Phoenix Experiment?"

I have, of course, never heard of such protocol, but I note down the number, believing it may aid me in any future confrontations with Cryptus. Or, for that matter, *any* AnthroMeta model.

"Certainly, Helmsman. I am required to tell the truth to my superiors."

Yeah, sure, pal, I think, once more recalling his withholding the truth about his memory of the blue pen. But I'm not his superior…

"Fine, Stygius," Oculus retorts, "but do it without exaggeration as well, if you don't mind. You-"

"Helmsman," Cryptus starts to interject.

The change in Oculus' voice and volume is surprising and jarring. "I am still speaking!" His veins pop out on his head, and there's an awkward silence where the air is so thick between them you could bake a cake in it. Oculus lets out a stabbing, quick sigh. "You used the word 'assault' when describing Jax's shaking you, yet you yourself struck him with your fist and he flew back. Do you deny this?"

"No, sir," Cryptus says, quietly.

Oculus' calm but irritated voice returns.

"Good. Then let us be clear. I need the facts and the truth please. No embellishment. Proceed," he growls, and the air is still thick.

Watching the two of them verbally joust, it suddenly becomes abundantly clear that there is a beef between them, and that they hardly see one another aboard this ship. Maybe that is on purpose. Clearly, there is no love lost between the two of them.

"I have the cerebro-print video file and can readily turn it over, if you wish to see it, Helmsman Oculus. You will see that there was nothing untoward conducted in Zaris Sharibian's session under my watch, which was her first aboard this ship. During the subject's session, she had just made contact with her parents.

"This was not her first time, Helmsman. Talicus reports she has previously enjoyed several successful rendezvous with her parents aboard The Zephyr. However, during this most recent session, the subject became overly preoccupied with," -here he pauses, strangely- "a *presence* inside her session. I can't describe it."

"A presence? What do you mean by that?" Oculus jabs.

I listen intently.

"That's just the thing, Helmsman, I do not know what it was." His face flickers momentarily, and I see it. I get the distinct sensation that he is lying. "The Phoenix Experiments exist to provide a communal bridge between the bereaved and the lost, for the betterment of our subjects, and-"

"Yes, yes, I know all this, Stygius," Oculus interrupts, and he's agitated, in no mood for any unnecessary reminders of Cryptus' function. "But go back to this, this, *presence,* if you please. Wasn't this just another banshee?"

Cryptus pauses, and then, remarkably, sighs. The action seems quite surprisingly human.

"No, Helmsman Oculus, it was not a banshee. And my capacity aboard this ship is to ensure the safety of all those onboard, especially those in my charge in the Phoenix Experiment program. Of course, dealing with the supernatural has its share of dangers, and you and I are all too familiar with what happened aboard the Rubris."

Ah, I think, *so the rumors of an incident aboard the Rubris* are *true.*

"Lest we have a repeat," Cryptus continues, "I must exercise caution and ensure that the subjects entrusted to me in the Phoenix Experiments are as safe as possible. Should they make contact with anything potentially dangerous or detrimental to our mission while connected, I must intervene. That is my primary program for our Phoenix Experiments here.

"Just such an incident occurred with Ensign Sharibian. Such an incident *nearly* occurred with Ensign Hutson here," he says, motioning to me.

My eyes squint at him, detecting his deceit. There was no such 'presence' in my session, at least, none that I recalled. It was my parents, and the fire, the noise, but very typical of banshees, nothing more.

"I do not know what this new presence was, but it was something nefarious, causing little Zaris great anxiety. And then," he trails off, and his eyes fall to the floor.

"Yes?" Oculus pries. "And then what…?"

"I- I can't be certain, Helmsman, but it seemed that we experienced some kind of… temporary *mesh*. Almost as if the apparition therein was seeking to exit the Phoenix Experiment through Zaris into our waking life here. Of course, I could *not* permit that. That is why I employed the use of my stasis interrupt pod."

So that's what that little zapper is called.

Oculus' face is crinkled into annoyance. He tilts his head. "What? A stasis interr-what?" he queries.

"Stasis interrupt pod. It is a small, cylindrical device meant to jolt the body back into a state of consciousness. Bring the subject back, as it were. It acts on the body's neural network, sleep drive, and circadian rhythm. I will admit that it is jarring, so I am grateful that I've never had to employ it."

I smirk and scoff. "That's not what you told me following our session! You told me that you've used it on everyone," I hiss through my teeth. "All the guys said that you haven't. That's when I knew that you *lied*."

As before, I make sure to add some extra emphasis to the last word in order for it to fully register with all present.

Cryptus doesn't respond to my allegation. He merely stares at Oculus and continues. "The stasis interrupt pod is a failsafe; a last-ditch recall device meant to shock the system and quickly retrieve the subjects from their subconscious state, restoring them to the natural world in the event of an emergency. Such an emergency was manifesting, and I needed to take effective measures to prevent a possible… *exit*."

"Wait," Mirabay interjects, "exit? Are you talking like 'demon possession' here? Is that what you're saying, Cryptus? It could possess Zaris?"

Again, a strange look on Oculus' face as he listens carefully to all of this. He clearly doesn't trust Oculus in this, and obviously thinks that all of this is pure nonsense.

Cryptus furrows his brow and clenches his lip, shaking his head vigorously. It is almost as if he is trying to purge the very thought from his brain. "Certainly not. Please understand, Mr. Mirabay, Mr. Oculus, and you too, Jax, that, as stated, I am unfamiliar with this presence. Before the females from The Zephyr boarded our ship, I had never encountered something so new, and so potentially hostile." His voice lowers to a menacing whisper as he stares directly at Oculus. "It is not of our physical plane, sir.

It is beyond the confines that we can see and touch. And it is *not* a banshee. A powerful force inhabits it, the likes of which I have never encountered, and nothing about it suggests benign or charitable intentions. On the contrary," he says, biting his lip, "I sense nothing short of malevolence."

"You sense nothing short of malevolence," Oculus repeats quietly, watching him skeptically. "And just what does malevolence feel like, Cryptus? I assume you know?" His voice has the bite of sarcasm to it.

Cryptus just regards him coldly. "Well, aside from the basic feeling registering as unease, hairs standing up on the back of your neck, sir, Jax here can attest easily enough to what little Zaris manifested at one point. I presume you've already told them, Jax?"

I glance at Oculus. The helmsman beats me to the punch. "What you reported to me about her eyes, and the sound she made, correct?" he asks, but his voice is steeped in mockery.

I nod.

Oculus suddenly rolls his eyes. "For the love… would you *please* give it a rest, you two. You're clearly at odds with each other. This is all outlandish ghost story nonsense. Enough! There's nothing definitive about any of this, Cryptus. How does her behavior in any way suggest malevolence?" Oculus' voice is permeated with irritation and incredulity. He clearly can't afford to be bothered with this, and has no intention of being so.

The synthetic turns to me once more, almost in a note of desperation. He speaks quietly. "Jax, have you told Oculus about the shape you saw in the-"

"I'm asking *you*, Cryptus," Oculus practically shouts again, and this time, he stands up with his hands on his hips. I'm taken aback. Oculus is clearly vexed, and wants straight answers from Cryptus.

"I don't expect either of you to imagine the fraying that helming such a massive ship can do to one's nerves since you've never been in command, Stygius Cryptus, but I've been out here a long time. We have enjoyed a smooth operation until now. But *now* I'm having to bear the responsibility for extra souls in my charge with these girls, *and* deal with the paranormal? This is bullswool! Hogwash, Cryptus."

Cryptus motions as if he's going to reply, but Oculus shuts him down, continuing his lecture.

"No! Wait your turn. I expected you to conduct the Phoenix Experiments with decorum, but you're turning them into a veritable freakshow. I've thought I was able to wholly entrust this to you, and I see now that I was in error."

As I watch all of this unfold, my trust in Oculus lessens. He's agitated to a breaking point, and I may have bitten off more than I can chew by getting Cryptus in trouble, I think. "I told him," I mutter to Cryptus, ignoring Oculus for the moment. "I started to see the shape."

Mirabay's eyes widen. "So something *was* actually starting to come through? Is that even possible?" he cries, turning to Oculus, though the helmsman is equally as bereft of answers as Mirabay.

"It *is* possible, indeed," Cryptus says, firmly, turning to Mirabay and appealing for reason since it seems Oculus has none. He speaks firmly. "That is one of the byproducts of the Phoenix Experiment, naturally: to allow, for example, Jax, here, to commune with his parents. If the communion is strong enough, and if those on the other side are willing to renounce their position in death, they could, feasibly, exit back into reality through the third chamber. That is precisely what it does. They could re-enter this life. But so could something else, sir. That is entirely the purpose of the experiments, to ultimately try to bring the parents back through, and to develop strong and capable Speakers to deal with the plague on Earth."

Oculus sighs thickly and puts his hands on his head, turning around in a full and annoyed revolution. He exhales heavily: a monstrous grunt of irascibility.

"Look, I've never pretended to understand your silly resurrection science, or what exactly the paranormal ramifications of it are, Stygius," he whines, "I've just sought to run a tight operation and a safe ship! Human or no, don't you think you have an obligation to inform your helmsman straightaway of even the *hint* of a possibility of a malevolent force seeking entry into The Origin through your accursed operation?"

"Sir, I meant no off-" Cryptus starts to say, and he stands, with his hands raised in defense.

"I don't care what you meant or didn't mean!" the helmsman barks, pointing at him. "Cryptus, you should have reported this *immediately*." He pauses, glancing over at Mirabay with a red, puffy face. "You leave me with little choice. As both a temporary measure *and* a consequence, I am effectively suspending the Phoenix Experiments until further notice pending a full investigation into this matter."

Cryptus, deflated, stands and begins to pace back and forth, passing in front of me and then heading back toward the entry to the ship's bridge. It's almost as if he's resigned to leave, muttering on his way out. "Sir, please don't. We cannot afford to susp-"

"My decision is final, *synthetic*," Oculus says, coldly. "Now sit the hell down. I did not give you permission to stand, much less leave. You are not dismissed until I say so, Stygius Cryptus."

Cryptus stops, momentarily balling his hands into fists, but he calms, turns, and stares at Oculus with icy regard. He salutes, but it's obviously halfhearted. The synthetic flashes a momentary glance in my direction, heaving another belabored sigh. Cryptus lifts his hands in defeat. "Fine. However, with your permission, helmsman, there's an added danger that I think you should be made aware of."

"I don't doubt it!" Oculus cries. "What do you know! Something *else* I haven't been made aware of in a timely fashion." He looks at me and rolls his eyes.

"It's not that nefarious, Helmsman. Please. May I approach and show you the Reference Video? I believe this will serve to reinforce your decision, which I will abide by, of course."

Mirabay shifts to my right.

Oculus rolls his eyes again and throws his hands up. "Fine. I presume this has to do with the Sharibian girl as well? Or are you about to spring yet another irritating surprise on me? The night is young, Cryptus."

Cryptus moves toward him. "Well, as I was saying, it's an added danger, certainly. But the danger is not from the girl, sir," he says.

"I don't understand," Oculus says, sitting down.

Cryptus moves to his right and hunches over the console in front of the helmsman. "It's from *you*," he says, and then my eyes twitch, not believing what I'm seeing.

With astonishing speed Cryptus sends a tightly coiled left fist backhandedly into Oculus' forehead. The helmsman reacts in surprise, grunting, his chair flying backward and his arms spasming outward in a reflex. In a horrifying revolution, Cryptus whirls around and with his right hand grabs Oculus' uniform at the neck, jerking him toward the ceiling, suspending all two hundred sixty pounds of him in the air.

Oculus nervously grasps for his throat to loosen the pressure and breathe, still in a stupor.

I jump to my feet.

"Cryptus, no!" I shout.

The synthetic pays me no heed.

Mirabay also rises in surprise, and dashes over to the console to defend his superior. "Jax, sit," he says coolly.

"Thank God, Argin – Mr. Mirabay – help him!" I cry. I extend my arms out in front of me, reaching in vain for Oculus.

I was never partial to him, but this is not only a breach of protocol; he appears to be in great pain, gasping for breath.

Cryptus doesn't show one ounce of remorse… or fatigue. The android suspends Oculus with his right hand, and our helmsman is still dazed. Cryptus' left hand is fishing for something in his pocket. Mirabay rushes toward both of them.

Except the First Officer doesn't defend Oculus.

Cryptus releases the helmsman suddenly, and Oculus plummets into his chair, flummoxed and striving to breathe. Mirabay retreats astern the helm chair, and yanks Oculus' arms back, pinning him.

Oculus cries out in pain as his arms are wrenched behind him.

"Do it," Mirabay says, coldly. "And be quick." He continues to restrain Oculus, who struggles to breathe, and attempts to say something, but he's gasping.

I watch in horror, not understanding what's happening, nor why. "No! What are you-"

A flash of light. A gleam of metal.

Cryptus whips out a small device that instantly periscopes into a serrated extension. Without a word, he mechanically slashes and stabs at the helmsman. My eyes widen as chills course through me. I want to vomit.

Mirabay has his head ducked down behind the seat, avoiding the hot splashes of blood pulsing out from Oculus' knifed body. Guttural cries and gulps sound from his deteriorating and perforated form as the life slowly ebbs from him.

The smell of iron fills the room.

Traces of blood splatter my uniform.

Cryptus is splashed and is now dripping with blood from the helmsman's body. Criss-crossing trails of red intersect Oculus' face, neck and chest as the android peels his skin open with each reddening stab and slash. Oculus' larynx practically falls forward out of his throat. His eyes are widened rings of white horror, gaping up at his assailant.

In a reflex, he bends his body toward his console, presumably to send out a ship-wide alert, but it's no use. He's not going anywhere.

But I am.

I can't see any more of it. I run. Faster than I've ever run before, I flee.

I hear Cryptus call for me from the bridge, but it's drowned out by the chills running down my flesh as I barrel through the halls of The Origin.

Helmsman Oculus is now dead, killed by our own synthetic, Stygius Cryptus. First Officer Argin Mirabay is accomplice to his murder.

I wonder where everyone is, and I don't even know where I'm at, but I struggle to think clearly and make for the rec hall. Before too long, I arrive, carried by the wind of my own fear.

They're all in here. All of them. Except for Zaris. However, their synthetic, Baryonnis Talicus, is with them as well. Where Zaris is, I don't know.

In a surprise, Venthix and Martos are here. Thankfully, their rec restriction is expired, and they're here with everyone else. For a brief second I wonder what Cryptus would do if he raced after me.

Would he kill me? Would he proceed to kill the rest of us? Such a morbid thought, but I don't put anything past Cryptus anymore, and I have no idea who is in charge between our synthetic and the murderous First Officer. They're obviously in league with each other.

My friends register my fright and stop what they're doing. I'm panting and going to drop. Yet, somehow, I press on.

"Cryptus… killed… Oculus. Mirabay… helped…" is all I can get out. I brace myself against a side column.

Their faces wring with horror and disbelief. Anther stares at me and slowly approaches. Ranshay is a study in confusion, as none of this makes sense to him through his language barrier.

Suddenly, a klaxon sounds throughout the ship.

"Anther, telling… the… truth. Help," I say, before falling into his arms. He catches me, staring into my eyes as he supports me, and he knows. He sees the truth in my horrified gaze, but he also notices the faint splatter of blood on my uniform.

My heart is beating like a rabbit, and fear has enveloped me entirely. I'm sweating and shivering through my shock.

Anther scrambles into gear, immediately. "Everyone, this way. Now! Come on, now! Orin, help!" he cries. All of them spring into action. A sudden panic settles upon everyone, pushed on by the emergency klaxon, but they fall in line, following us toward the far end of the rec hall away from the main doors.

Anther turns to Talicus. "Baryonnis, you've got to disable Phiria's security surveillance right away. Video *and* audio surveillance. He can't see or hear where we are. Encode it with your own. Trust me."

"I can, certainly. They can always reboot the surveillance servers, but they would have to physically be in the server room to do that. Access code?"

"Bravo-Zulu-September-Niner-Three-One-Tango."

I hear it, but I'm amazed and surprised at the existence of the code, why Anther would have access to such a thing, nor where he appropriated it. Perhaps he had done more exploring and spying in this ship than I ever gave him credit for. Perhaps he had even spied on the girls showering. We would get to that later, and I briefly hope he'll share with me the best points to view from. But somewhere along the line, like a forager, he harvested this important code.

For now, Talicus complies.

The synthetic turns her head forward and closes her eyes, yet continues to run without fail alongside us. She doesn't need her eyes open to see. She communicates with Phiria wirelessly, sending the code.

And somewhere, in the ship's central computer servers, the surveillance grid goes offline.

"Done," she confirms. "I've programmed in a backdoor to allow me to input my own code if the servers get rebooted. That way I can restart the process if need be, later."

Anther regards her and senses the job is done. "We just bought ourselves some time. At least they won't be able to track us to our first destination. Hopefully, they won't see us somewhere else after that. Then, it's a game of cat and mouse, baby."

We run.

All of us.

Into the vents at the end of the rec hall. Like moles burrowing underground, we disappear from site, leaving behind the murderous Cryptus, Mirabay, and, somewhere in this ship, little Zaris. I hope to God she'll be alright. The chiefs aren't here either; from our ship or The Zephyr. Where they are, I have no idea, but they are also now in grave danger.

We can't save everyone, I think to myself.

We run. Quietly, surreptitiously, we snake our way into the bowels of the ship, Anther leading us on to safety somewhere. I wonder what they're doing back on the bridge. I wonder if they're hiding Oculus' body and coming up with an alibi of sorts.

It doesn't matter. Our helmsman is dead, and we're now at the mercy of a sentient synthetic tied into our entire ship in ways I can't even pretend to understand. I only hope that Talicus grasps his murderous inclinations and can match him in intellect and strength. What I saw Cryptus do to our helmsman defies belief, and I have no idea if Talicus is his equal.

I find myself thinking I should have taken more note of the punch Cryptus doled out, reckoning with his strength earlier. That might have given me sense enough to not challenge him.

Anther helps me along, propping me up. I feel another body to my left, and a sweet fragrance envelops me. "Hang in there, Jax. We've got you."

The truth is known now, naked, cold
The toll exacting, though 'twas bold

> *Now sides are drawn,*
> *no time to fawn*
> *As peril grows amidst the fold*
>
> *Of those who knoweth painful real*
> *Of them who wouldest safety steal*
> *For evil lurketh,*
> *malice worketh*
> *And Phoenix riseth all surreal*

I hear the voice and register the words. I don't know what they mean, and I don't care. Everything is now changed, but what I wouldn't give for one quick kiss to make the horror and shock dissipate into the ether.

I look over at Alaris, into her beautiful eyes, stumbling along the ground.

PART TWO:
Into the Fire

9: The Opposition

The voice is jarring, and we all hear it.

"All personnel to the Assembly Hall please. All personnel to the Assembly Hall."

It's Phiria, but the words come from Cryptus, and I know it. He's not fooling anyone, and no one here wants to take the chance of trusting him following my report.

In my heart, I know the chiefs are going to meet Cryptus and Mirabay there. What they will decide to tell them about Oculus… about us… I have no idea. Perhaps in desperation, I hope that our chiefs Bannitor and Ambrosius will be able to suss out what happened, and figure out the truth of the matter. Hopefully, they'll survive this.

We reach Quadrant G, Subfloor 6B, and I sit down and tell everyone what happened, as best as I can given my memory, which has been afflicted by shock. I can't see straight, frankly, and all I can do is shake my head over and over again in incredulity. Everything happened so fast and so violently, I had little time even to run.

Their questions mostly deal with the First Officer.

Why would Mirabay do that?

Mirabay was in on it?

How on earth could Mirabay betray Oculus?

I have no answers. I don't know what to say. Once we sit, someone hands me water. I practically guzzle down the entire bottle. Thankfully, they don't pepper me with questions as I gulp it down between breaths.

The conversation falls to a hush. I look around.

No chiefs Marxim Bannitor or Hin Ambrosius. Our chiefs are missing; on their way to meet the conspirators. No female chiefs Ashira Sarristo or Maridie Onyx either. Just us kids. Except…

…no little Zaris. Greeting me warily – and with a clear trace of nervousness – I look the rest of them in the eyes in fear.

Orin. Strong and muscular. His muscles will be needed.

Ranshay. Poor little Ranshay doesn't even understand what's going on. That makes two of us, regardless of the language barrier.

Venthix.

Martos.

Garris.

Dravin.

Alaris.

Omnias.

Donetis.

Raelia.

Skarbé.

Ghirisha.

Miritia.

Baryonnis Talicus, our synthetic.

That's sixteen of us, altogether. Sixteen against two murderers, with one of them possessing superhuman strength and supreme intellectual cunning.

And now, we wait.

There is quiet chatter amongst some of them. I watch Alaris as she huddles close to her girlfriends and whispers unintelligible secrets to them, and they to her. I can only assume that they're all resenting their changed circumstances and dreading their stay onboard our ship.

I look at Orin. He is, after all, the oldest of us. Though our new synthetic demonstrates the ability to help in disabling the surveillance, I'm almost as unsure of her as I am of Cryptus. I want human help, *thankyouverymuch.* Orin will do nicely.

"Orin, what do we do?" I ask. "Do you think we should try to find our chiefs, and rally them to our cause? We're all alone down here."

Raelia shivers. So does Miritia, but Orin puts his arm around her and draws her close to himself.

"I dunno, Jax," he says. "It might be worth a shot, but hell if *I* wanna go back up there. We've gotta think about food, water, maybe even setting up some kind of barricade or something. I mean, do you have any idea why Cryptus would just flip like that?"

"Maybe we should call him 'Fliptus' from now on," Anther jokes. I don't find it funny. No one laughs.

I shake my head. "No idea. It was all so sudden and unexpected. Oculus was getting angrier and more irritated, and his voice was raised. The way that Cryptus just… *turned*… I didn't see it coming. And I certainly didn't see Mirabay doing what he did."

"Yeah, that's cold. So cold!" Venthix exclaims.

Ranshay's eyes bounce back and forth between all of us. He has no clue what's going on.

Orin decides to help.

"Talicus, can you interpret for Ranshay here please? We'd all like to know precisely what led up to this as well. Jax, do you mind?"

"Certainly. I'll do whatever I can," Talicus says. I nod my head. She surprises us all by literally removing her left ear, rotating it counterclockwise, and then detaching it from her head. She holds it up to Ranshay's right ear like it's some kind of wireless speaker, and he listens.

Slowly, the chatter dies down amongst all of them as I gather breath into my lungs. I recount what Omnias and I saw with Zaris in the Phoenix Experiment. How it unnerved and scared us. How Cryptus lied to me following my finally discovering my parents in there. How Zaris flipped out at me in the rec hall.

How I decide to talk to Oculus. How Anther warns me not to, and how I realize now that I should have taken his words more to heart. How Cryptus shows up in the bridge and he says I assaulted him, and how I inform Oculus about the android punching me.

How he and Oculus argue. How Cryptus explains about the new phenomenon, the 'presence' as he calls it, and how Oculus doesn't want to hear about his 'silly science.' And then, the awful moment when Cryptus and Mirabay murder him.

Talicus interprets everything for Ranshay into Hindi in near real-time. We all hear it coming through her dismembered left ear in a tinny fashion, but Ranshay understands everything. His little brown face scrunches up in worry as she translates. Ranshay's eyes grow steadily wider, and at one point his mouth falls open in dismay. His eyes dart between me and Talicus as he listens intently. He fires the occasional question of verification. I hear him say *hatya?* after Talicus informs him that Oculus has been murdered. She nods, and continues.

She ends somberly, seeming to reflect the gravity of our situation. Ranshay looks around himself in nervous apprehension, perhaps wondering if the area we've taken temporary refuge in is, in fact, safe. I wonder the same thing.

I glance around at the nervous faces. They have now heard the story in full as well, in their own language. It wasn't any easier for them hearing it as it was for Ranshay, nor Talicus, I'll wager. But now they all know the awful truth, at last.

Ghirisha voices the first question. "I had no idea that's what the Phoenix Experiments were for. I thought they were just to help us commune with our parents, or anyone else that we've lost. I thought it was to make us better Speakers for our return to Earth! It can actually bring our parents back to life?"

The others nod.

"Yep. And I thought so too," I say. "I think that it's still for Speakers, sure, but I didn't know about this- this *presence* thing."

"Does Cryptus really think that something was trying to come through?" asks Martos, and he looks like he considers all of this just ridiculous fiction.

"I have no idea *what* Cryptus thinks, Martos." I say with a bit of heat. "Not anymore. He was always so… remote… but this was just unexpected and over the top."

Martos nods and shuts up.

Talicus continues interpreting for Ranshay, but she interjects a thought. "It is, of course, a foregone conclusion that many or perhaps all of you might be somewhat nervous in my company. I completely understand. At the top of an AnthroMeta model's primary protocol is, of course, the prohibition against harming humans. Self-preservation is at the very top."

"Cryptus mentioned that," I mutter.

"Nonetheless, I want to assure you I have no such directives or programming to harm any of you. I neither approve of nor understand my colleague's behavior and rash actions. He is quite obviously operating outside normal AnthroMeta parameters. Please rest assured that I will do my utmost to protect all of you girls and boys."

I study her. "Do you have the same strength that Cryptus has?"

She nods. "It comes standard in our models."

"What model number are you?" Anther asks her. She turns to him. Ranshay is still holding her detached ear up to his, and his head swivels between all of us.

"AnthroMeta Model K300 Series C."

I furrow my brow. "Wait – you're more advanced than Cryptus?"

She nods. "Yes. By 2.16 generations, in fact."

"So, if it came down to fighting him, you could beat him?" continues Anther.

"Theoretically. Let us hope it does not come to that. My cybernetic strength protocols are for last resort use only," she says. She offers an unsettlingly saccharin smile.

This model obviously doesn't approve of violence. Fine, I think to myself. But Cryptus assured me of the same thing, yet I saw what he did to Oculus. It was nothing short of savage, despite his promise.

And just then, the voice comes once more, whispering to me out of nowhere:

Trust may vanish, fidelity fleet
Giving no rise for harmony meet
　　　But conscience begs
　　　to give faith legs
Co-laboring together in fiery heat

Now cannot live craven doubt
Lest vanity preclude the faithful, stout
　　　So stalwart rise,
　　　stare fear down eyes
Laden with faith to wariness rout

With that, I decide to try to trust Talicus. There's something about her that is markedly different from Cryptus, of course, notwithstanding the fact that she's never murdered someone in front of me.

At that precise moment, watching her, I find myself wishing that my Phoenix session could have gone on just a bit longer. I had *almost* reached them. I was *that* close. What I wouldn't give for a brief embrace in the midst of that fiery inferno. Cryptus denied me that before he ultimately denied Oculus his life. I decide resolutely that it would be too much to deny Talicus a measure of trust.

It's not a huge stretch After all, she has already proven herself faithful by disabling the surveillance on the way here.

"Jax. Jax, you still with us?" Anther snaps his fingers in front of my face, and I startle.

"Huh? Yeah. Sorry. Thanks, Talicus. Ant," I say, turning my attention to him, "you've been around the ventilation shafts more than I have, I think. Where should we go? We can't just walk around through the corridors."

"I'm hungry," whines Raelia.

Anther registers what she says. "Well, yeah, there's that. We could swing through the storage supplies and grab some tasty *BioPrime* for a pick-me-up. And I have to wizz too. Anyone else gotta wiz?"

"Crude, but yes," Alaris replies. "We have to, uh, 'wizz' soon as well."

"What about the rumor of the Engineer?" I ask him, disregarding the toilet talk.

"The Engineer?" he asks me quizzically.

"Yeah, there's someone down there keeping things running and going back and forth doing checkups. We've never met them. But The Origin's manifest and readouts always display one count higher than the occupants I've ever seen walking around. It's been 'us-plus-one,' though they are unnamed in the system."

"I've heard of her too," Venthix says. "The rumors are that it's a woman. We could try to find her. Maybe she can help us navigate the ship better, and find more ways to hide from them."

"Yeah, but," Orin argues, "is that all we're going to be doing now? Running around and hiding? We can't live like that. Cryptus needs to be confronted – and stopped."

"Yeah. Mirabay too," voices little Dravin, quiet as a mouse up until this point.

We're all lost in thought, wondering where we should go and what we should do now.

"If I may," Talicus interrupts, "I think you're wise to seek out the help of the Engineer. If for no other reason than to keep her safe from Cryptus and Mirabay as well, but it would be prudent to seek her counsel as to threading your way throughout the ship. She may also have ways to communicate with others and recruit help."

"Yeah," voices Donetis, "we really need to tell The Rubris to back off. To not come here. They would be in danger too!"

I confess I had forgotten about The Rubris. We definitely should contact them and alert them to what has happened aboard The Origin.

"I don't know," Orin argues, "that might be catastrophic for us, you guys. We tell them, they turn back, and we're stuck here with Cryptus."

"Yeah, but if we let them come here, Cryptus or Mirabay might kill them and take control of their ship too!" Donetis fires back.

Orin shakes his head. "I think they'd come prepared, don't you guys? We tell them what's up, they get some weapons, they come here and force Cryptus and Mirabay to stand down."

Miritia nods her head and stares affectionately at Orin as if to say *my hero*...

I seize the moment to roll my eyes noisily.

"Yeah but they're a *long* way off, Orin," I point out. "They're over a year away! We have to find someone else, someone much closer to The Origin."

"There were repair crews en route to The Zephyr prior to her detonation," Talicus says. "They were turned back. I recommend we send a message to them, informing them of our situation and stating emphatically that we have need of them."

I look around. Everyone seems to be nodding. Except for Raelia, who only looks emphatically hungry.

"Orin? You agree?" I ask him.

He nods.

"They're the closest. Do you know if they're armed, Talicus?"

"I'm sorry," she replies. "I have no knowledge as to their armament or skill other than ship repair."

"Well, even if they have welding torches, that'll be something," Orin says, standing. "Well, let's get to it. Raelia is hungry, and Anther has to wizz. I'm sure they're not the only ones, either. Talicus, can you pull up a schematic of the ship and tell us the best route down to maintenance?"

Anther looks deflated at this request. "I know the way. I can guide us."

"No, let Talicus tell us the way, Ant."

Anther's eyebrows dip down and his jaw clenches. "Don't call me that. Anyway, who died and made you the leader?" he asks defensively.

"I'm the oldest, Anther," Orin says, and he looks defiant. Miritia's eyebrows go up, ready to defend her new partner.

"Technically, *I* am the oldest here," Talicus says. "If anyone should be in command, it should be the smartest, strongest, *and* the oldest. I am, of course, all three."

Orin's eyes dart over at her, appraising her. He appears to be sizing her up for the task. I feel the same way. I'm not entirely sure I want a synthetic leading us, but I relent. The poetic voice still resounds in my head.

Orin sighs, looks around, and then his eyes land on Miritia. She throws up a quick, indifferent eyebrow, seeming to relent.

"Alright, fine, Talicus," Orin says. "Since you're, ya know, the smartest, strongest, *and* the oldest," he mocks. "You lead. What's the plan?"

Talicus wastes no time, consumed neither by ego nor any kind of scorekeeping. She's simply following her programming – the programming that Cryptus referred to.

Self-preservation is our overriding protocol, just as it is for humans.

"I think the recommendation to proceed to the engine room, through the ventilation shafts and ducts, makes sense. We will stop by the food supply on the way to replenish. There are sixteen of us, and we all need to keep up with each other. I suggest Anther leads the way to the engine room, and I will confirm his trajectory."

Anther turns and smiles heartily at Orin in victory.

"Once we have arrived there," Talicus continues, "we will ascertain the location of the Engineer. Meanwhile, I have already contacted the repair ship Achilles and informed them of our situation. They are preparing a response as we speak, so we have that working for our benefit."

I stare at her. "You did that already?"

She blinks. "Yes. I record in real-time, and a transcription of our conversation has been provided to them, along with a summary of what you describe happened on the bridge with your helmsman and First Officer."

"Wow," I say. "That's… impressive."

Talicus smiles.

The others look impressed as well.

"Nonsense," she replies briskly. "I'm a synthetic. Top of the line. We're efficient and effective."

Yeah. At running Phoenix experiments and killing helmsmen, I think, but I keep it to myself.

She starts to move. "Anther, if you please? Go on ahead of me and lead on. I'll check you if you stray off the trajectory. I assume you're aware of the junction ahead? Make a-"

"Left. I know," Anther says, as he looks back with a cocky smile. "I'm a human. Top of the line. We're efficient and effective," he says with a smirk.

"Excellent," she says.

"I think we should hurry," Omnias says. "If they're not hurting Zaris, they might use her."

"For what?" Alaris asks her.

"To bring that presence through." She gulps, and we all hear it.

The very notion makes us all look at each other in horror for a moment, but we resign to push on. No one wants to be stuck in ventilation shafts with a malevolent presence onboard.

Another klaxon sounds overhead, followed by another announcement sounding throughout the ship.

"Now hear this, now hear this, Helmsman Oculus here, please report to the Assembly Hall at once. All crew and passengers of The Origin, please report to the Assembly Hall at once. Last call."

This time we jump and look at each other in surprise. I know in my heart, and my eyes and memory confirm it, that our helmsman is dead. I was there. Cryptus killed him himself. That leaves only one explanation. I shake my head and let everyone see me doing so. *It's a lie,* I say with my mind.

That was Cryptus' voice.

My heart goes out to all souls aboard this ship who don't know of his sinister actions, and the only malevolent force I can readily identify aboard The Origin belongs not to an unknown presence, but to Cryptus himself.

His voice is jarring again, and we all heard it.

10: The Stranger

Our hearts grow lighter the further we get into this titanic ship.

We're deep in the underbelly of The Origin now. We've all heard nothing further from either Phiria nor Cryptus, nor Cryptus impersonating anyone. In conversation, it's clear we're all apprehensive of any further overhead communications, perhaps even more than rounding a corner and inadvertently coming face to face with the murderous synthetic himself.

We've gone now for an hour, all sixteen of us carefully threading our way through the vents and shafts, keeping as quiet as we can. Along the way I ask Talicus if there's a chance Cryptus might shut her out of Phiria and prevent further access to the ship's onboard AI.

"It's certainly possible, but it's unlikely, Ensign Hutson," she replies, "as Phiria is a fellow sentient, and she would need clear and concise reasons, as well as authorization codes from the ship's helmsman to restrict access. The helmsman is now deceased, of course, and can issue no such codes. That leaves concise reasons, and I've already confirmed with Phiria that she has witnessed – and recorded – the attack and slaying of Fulsar Oculus. She has subsequently taken the initiative to demote Stygius Cryptus and restrict his access. He and Mirabay have been demoted."

Well, that's good to know, I think. Having safeguards in place to prevent Cryptus from locking out Talicus gives me some reassurance.

We're close to the engine room, and the deep throbbing grows steadily as we press onward. We've all managed to pee somewhere or other – finding places to urinate off the beaten path was an interesting task – and Venthix, Martos and little Dravin found the supply room and commandeered several dozen packs of BioPrime and bottled water for our group to share. Thankfully, they also had the good sense to grab a bag to carry everything in.

So, that is now taken care of.

Now we just need to find this rumored Engineer that supposedly runs around in the dark down here, God only knows why.

"Time for a break, with your permission, of course, Talicus," Orin says, deferring to her with a bit of a snotty sarcasm. She nods. "I confess my legs are tired, and everyone's panting and sweating."

Indeed, down in the depths of The Origin, it's hot and stuffy. Thankfully, most everyone was dressed lightly up in the rec hall where I found them, as our uniforms would be stifling. I know mine is. Alaris is right beside me, and she's glistening. Every so often I catch her looking longingly at me, as if she's remembering that kiss. I know I am.

We all sit down slowly, creaking at the knees as we've been crawling through this God-forsaken ship. Everyone sighs to varying degrees. Moans are plentiful as we all massage our sore joints and palms.

"Talicus," I ask, "what's the ETA on the Achilles? Can you monitor communication with them and determine their status?"

"One moment," she replies, and becomes very still. It's always creepy when she connects to Phiria that way. "They appear to be prepping for launch as we speak. ETA 2 hours and 14 minutes."

"That's a long time," I sigh. "Can Cryptus turn them around? Redirect them, I mean?"

Talicus shakes her head. The perimeters of her corneas briefly flash blue as she disconnects from

Phiria. "I had taken the liberty of informing them of the saboteurs onboard. They are under instruction not to comply with any new directives from Stygius Cryptus or Argin Mirabay due to their demotions. I've invoked AnthroMeta Primary Protocol 2D."

We all stop short, waiting. It's like she doesn't know that we're not well-versed in AnthroMeta protocols.

"Sorry," she continues, seeing our expressions, "it establishes a synthetic hierarchy that places me in a position of supremacy and precludes anyone else's directives from interfering with my primary objectives."

"So, like, whenever you wanted, you could have basically taken over the entire ship?" Orin asks. "Talk about a synthetic coup d'etat!"

"Theoretically, yes," Talicus says. "Phiria would still need to contact Earth headquarters for the approval, but yes."

"And what *are* your primary objectives?" Alaris asks her, point blank.

"To ensure the survival of all of you, and the continuation of the Phoenix Experiments as soon as humanly possible."

Most of us nod, thankful to hear that. As long as it's true, of course. Everyone is sprawled out now, either sitting or lying down, and chugging water. Donetis pours a bit of her water bottle down her back, arching in response, but clearly invigorated by the sensation of the cooling fluid. She moans in pleasure.

"What about the Achilles?" Garris asks, trying to ignore the inadvertent seductive display. "What happens when they try to dock with us?"

A highly reasonable question.

"I had not thought that far through the process," Talicus says stoically. "I am sorry. I'm still working through calculations of theoretical scenarios and appropriate responses. Most likely, we can expect interference from Cryptus and Mirabay, and possibly the chiefs – *if* they've sided with them."

I realize then that I had forgotten about the chiefs. All four of them. Whether they have sided with Cryptus or have been killed is unknown to all of us. Time will tell, of course.

"Why would the chiefs side with Cryptus?" Miritia asks Talicus. "And why wouldn't he just kill them too?"

"I am, as yet, unaware as to the rationale or purposes of my colleague, so, for the time being, I cannot speculate as to his motives," Talicus replies, and then she looks up and meets Miritia's eyes. "Or the fate of the four chiefs."

"Yeah, well, as for me, I think it's about time we found this supposed Engineer, if she even exists. It seems she might be the only one we can trust, especially if she didn't report to the Assembly Hall. Oculus did order *all* crew and passengers to report."

"*Cryptus* ordered that," I say. "Let's be clear."

"Whatever," Miritia bites back. "You know what I mean." She blows hot, wet hair out of her face and rolls her eyes. "We need to find that Engineer, like, *now*."

"And what will you do with her, once you find her?" utters an elderly voice, scratchy and raspy, laden with a thick Mexican accent.

A few of the girls shriek in alarm. Nearly all of us jump to our feet and whirl around to face the mysterious voice.

Our hearts are seized with fear once more.

Blending into the shadows behind us, formless against the dark of the vast walls of machinery and tubing, conduits, vents and cabling, a shape shifts slightly. None of us sees her coming, nor knows how long she has stood there listening to us.

We wait. There comes a soft, grim laugh.

Talicus sweeps some of the girls who were in front of her to a safer position behind her. "Identify yourself, please," she says coldly to the newcomer.

The figure doesn't move, but the voice returns. "Have you not guessed my identity already? Surely there is no one else down here to suggest an alternate persona?"

I watch her. Instantly I know who it is.
"You're the Engineer. Right?" I ask, tilting my head and slowly advancing toward her.

She doesn't answer, but I can practically feel her smiling at me, regarding me from the darkened bowels of The Origin.

"Am I?" the voice finally utters. "Only you can tell."

"What does that mean?"

The voice grunts, and the figure shifts.

"Halt," says Talicus, stoically once more, forming a precautionary screen between the woman and us. "Do not advance until you are properly identified. I am requesting this cordially. I will not ask again, and will be required to use force."

The woman pays her no heed.

She slowly steps out into the light, and the faint amber glow from the ceiling falls upon her diminutive, elderly form.

Our jaws drop.

I was right: she is elderly, and definitely of Latino blood. She's only perhaps four and a half feet tall, wearing an oil-streaked dirty gray jumpsuit, the black wisps of her hair clasped neatly into some kind of clamp behind her head. She is wearing thick, black-rimmed glasses, but they don't fit her. They're generic, and her pupils are grossly enlarged behind them, studying us.

But for her sweet, maternal smile, I do believe that Talicus may have attacked her. Then, we all might be running from *two* androids.

She just stands there, everyone surveying her, and she surveying everyone.

"Who are you?" I ask her, but I can hear – and feel – the timidity in my own voice. Alaris clutches my arm as I am slowly, inadvertently drawn toward the stranger.

"There's no need to be alarmed. My name is Rosie," the old lady breathes. "And in answer to your question, yes, I am the Engineer. Sorry if I was coy. I've been down here a long time and, well," -here she dons a rather embarrassed expression, "I don't get many visitors."

"H-how long have you been down here?" I ask.

Ranshay nervously points to her and tugs on Talicus' arm. The android detaches her ear once more and gives it to Ranshay so that he can understand.

Rosie frowns. "This may come as a shock to you, but I actually don't know. I guess, an Engineer is typically expected to keep tabs on all the machinery and ensure functionality, check for abnormalities, keep things ship-shape. I actually don't have much mastery of any of those abilities, however."

"Rosie," Talicus echoes. "You are Rosalita Dahlia Campion, is that your full name?"

"It is indeed," she says. "You are Baryonnis Talicus, AnthroMeta model K300, yes? And you are Ensign Jax Hutson," Rosie says to me. She looks around at all of us individually. "I know who all of the boys are. The girls I'm just now getting acquainted with through ship's records since your arrival on The Origin. I'm so sorry about your own ship and mates. My condolences on the loss of the Zephyr crew and passengers," she frowns. "I'm able to keep tabs on what goes on up top through the terminals down here. Your names were on a manifest," she says in a nod to the girls.

"Why didn't you respond to Oculus' summons to the Assembly Hall?" I ask her, intentionally using our helmsman's name even though it was clearly Cryptus impersonating him. "He specifically instructed all crew to report."

Rosie cocks an eyebrow. "Because I don't report to synthetics, Mr. Hutson, present company excluded." Talicus bows graciously. "Especially those who slay their superiors."

Now my eyebrow raises. "So you know what happened on the bridge?"

"I do."

"So… so…," my words fail me, caught between gratitude that she knew and could possibly aid us, and confusion over how an elderly woman could even render aid, "what do we do, Rosie? You've been here a long time, you know this ship, what do we do?"

She laughs grimly again, shaking her head. "Well, judging by what I've seen, young Anther here knows this ship much better than I do, and his knees are arguably in better shape for crawling through air ducts. Less noisy creaking of joints."

Anther chuckles.

"And yes, the horror - though I've never even met Helmsman Oculus, no one should die like that. I did happen to read what happened through Phiria.

Thank you for the succinct update, Baryonnis. I appreciate it."

"You are most welcome, Rosalita."

"Just Rosie will do," Rosie says, laughing graciously. "Now, as to your question, young Jax, I think what you've all done, coming down here, was wise. I am on your side, please know that. And by summoning the Achilles here to help, I would call that a measure of wisdom as well. I think you should all stay down here with me until we all figure this whole sordid situation out."

There's a moment of pause while we all somberly appraise the situation. I must confess that Rosie's presence – elderly and maternal – conveys a measure of tangible and felt hope. Glancing around at all of us, it looks like that hope is shared by everyone here. There's something about her: a power; perhaps a degree of intangibility or… something. She seems far older than her elderly form… ageless… I can't quite put my finger on it. I'm not scared or threatened by it, and I find her incredibly interesting. *Maybe even more than Alaris,* I think to myself.

"Now, take heart, everyone, because there's one more thing," Rosie says, and something in the way that she says this makes me frown. Her tone of voice changes; the tangible feeling of hope is punctured like a balloon.

"I have been watching, and listening, and even praying. I know about the missing passenger, young Zaris Sharibian. And I know what your android was doing." She pauses, awkwardly. "I guess there's no easy way to say this." Rosie gathers her breath, surveying all of us somberly. "Jax, Omnias, you weren't off in your suspicion. A dreadful presence is in those Phoenix Experiments that you do. Something horrible. Something deeply malignant and hostile.

"It is something I had never encountered in my long, storied life here. I don't know what your android has been doing, but the incident with little Zaris was only the beginning, I fear.

"This… thing," she says, shaking her head and staring at the ground, "is hellbent on breaking free of its captivity and entering our world. It seeks to do so through a vulnerable host. And little Zaris is still with your android. I fear for her safety. I fear for all of our safety. It wants her. It wants you. And we must *not* give ourselves over to it."

I can't wait any longer. I want to know what the thing was inside the third chamber. And perhaps in my own session with Cryptus before he zapped me out. "Rosie, what *is* the presence?"

"I don't know what it might be called on the other side. But this side of death, it is called The Djinn. It is an ancient evil, and it must *never* come through."

A cold shiver runs down my spine, and my arms are dotted with bumps.

Alaris leans into me, and I feel her trembling.

Fear not, children, for thy deranger

Comes not through this present stranger
Keep thy faith
Fear not thy wraith
Forsake not prudence for clear danger

We all lean into her. Rosie's face twists into knots as she conjures up the words to describe the evil she's witnessed. As I briefly look around, my friends huddle closer together, seeking companionship and warmth amidst such cold, terrifying revelations.

"The Djinn are supernatural entities from Islamic and pre-Islamic Arabian myth. But they are no myths, children. Not anymore. Spirits composed of smokeless fire, they exist alongside us. I have encountered only one, but it is enough. They are invisible shapeshifters, they can influence us, possess us, and cause mental illness."

"Where do they come from?" Omnias asks. I see the look on her face, and it's stoic. She remembers what we both started to see forming in the third chamber during Zaris' session.

"I do not know," Rosie answers. "They are not immortal, but they do have lengthy lifespans. Once they have found a possible exit, they will *not* leave. They are malevolent and wicked to the core, and they cause great fear. The Djinn is the worst entity I have ever encountered, far worse than banshees."

"How do you know all of this?" Talicus asks her. "And how long have you known?"

Rosie glances up at her. "I've only just learned of its intensity. It is nothing to trifle with, and, even now, Stygius Cryptus is toying with something incomparably evil up there, and if it gets out…," she trails off. *If it gets out,*" she mutters once more, leaving us leaning into her as she cocks an eyebrow.

That doesn't help. I want her to finish that sentence. "If it gets out, *what* exactly, Rosie?"

She looks at me. A solemn expression wraps her face as she gathers her breath.

"It will be the end. This thing is from the other side, and it has no business here. It does not belong."

"How do you know that?" Anther prods.

Rosie smiles gently, as if consumed by some memory that long predates any of us. Her eyes stare into the wells of space, possessed by reflection.

"Because I don't belong, either. It – and I – have been there," she says. "On the *other* side."

We just stare at her.

"I'm no longer living," she clarifies.

Rosie was dead once?

That can mean only one thing.

She returned through the Phoenix Experiment. Perhaps in a session with only Cryptus present? But why would she be down here, and why bring her back in the first place?

And if she came back, so could my parents… right?

But if she can come through, and they can come through, that means that something *else* could possibly come through as well.

Poor little Zaris. I realize with horror that she will be used as the conduit… the portal through which Cryptus will unleash this dreadful presence. A shiver runs through me.

My heart grows heavier the further I get into these frightening truths.

11: The Truth

As if on the coattails of an introduction, right on cue, we hear it.

How can we *not* hear it?

The horrifying cry resonates throughout the entire ship, stopping all our hearts at once. It grows in intensity until we cover our ears.

Ripples run down my flesh as thrills of fear wash over me. I grip Alaris close to me and send my frightened eyes all around, scanning the corridors, the ceiling, everything, wary of the approaching menace.

An unearthly growl rumbles throughout the ship, burgeoning in intensity and pitch until it bounces off every single wall, reverberating throughout every corridor, rising to a howling scream of wind and wrath. Sucking our very courage from us, it saps every last bit of hope into a vortex of trepidation.

"Something is happening in Quadrant C, Subfloor 3A," Talicus says, apparently unfazed by the noise. "Phiria reports a massive volume differential, and an unknown presence detected."

"It's The Djinn," Rosie says, her eyes shut tight. "We must move. Now."

"Oh, no!" Omnias wails. "What does that mean for Zaris, Rosie?"

Rosie, who had started to move down the corridor to lead us on, looks straight at her. "Your friend Zaris is dead. There is nothing you can do now except flee. Do *not* be afraid. Follow me."

And with that, Rosie takes off at astonishing pace, the rest of the sixteen of us falling in behind her in no particular order.

> *Gather not thy weapons useless*
> *Tether not thy cunning ruthless*
> *Dark dawn cometh,*
> *terror mammoth*
> *Rendering thy vain hope fruitless*

We're finally moving slower now, all of us, threading our way further into the belly of The Origin. Rosie says nothing. She leads us on with determination, and Talicus falls in step behind her. Orin and Miritia are next, followed by Anther and Omnias, the rest of the girls, and then the boys and I take up the rear. I can't shake a feeling of creeping dread behind me as I push on, waiting for some primal force to seize me from behind and engulf me.

But Rosie seems to know what she's doing, and she's taking us somewhere: silently, wordlessly, we're now entirely in her hands.

There is one more ghostly roar right after we begin to flee, and then, suddenly, an eerie silence where we can all hear each other breathing. Every tiny shifting of weight, every tendon flexing, every blink: we hear it, amplified in these dark corridors with the terror of our hearts pounding in our ears.

At intervals, we hear reports throughout the ship, some dull concussion against the greater overwhelming din of engines and thrusters and God knows what else rumbles down here to make The Origin go. No one says anything to anyone else, but glances are exchanged, and in those glances, nothing but nervousness and fear.

We've now descended down endless shafts, scaled ladders, filed singly through trap doors and chutes, and even slid one-by-one down some spillway to a waiting room below, throbbing with intense sound. I figure we have got to be somewhere near the reactor room, accounting for all the noise.

I slowly make my way up to Anther, passing the other boys and girls. I need to talk to him. The Djinn is somewhere up on the higher floors. Up there with Cryptus, the chiefs, and Zaris. *No- wait- not Zaris. Not anymore,* I think to myself. *Dammit, Cryptus, you traitor. You let one through.*

"Hey buddy," I say. "Wher-"

Anther startles, looking at me with eerie, widened eyes white with panic as I suddenly appear unexpectedly to his left. He clutches his heart. "Dude! Don't do that!" he whispers. "Scared the crap out of me." He tosses an embarrassed look at Omnias, who says nothing to his right.

"Sorry. Where are we?"

He shakes his head. "I've lost track. I know we're in Quadrant H or I, and we're probably on Subfloor 12 or 13 now, I think. Hard to tell. I've never ever been down this far, Jax. It's hot and quiet. And dark," he finishes, and I can tell he has an intense distaste for the word, given our circumstances.

Suddenly a thought comes to me, and it's a macabre one. "The Origin," I say, shaking my head. Anther looks over at me, confused. "What a name for a ship that has become a portal for a supernatural entity. It's almost like it was fate." Anther doesn't reply, lost in thought. We trudge on, but I can't help but ruminate now about The Zephyr and the Rubris: what they were named for. I think *zephyr* means something like a breeze, but I have no idea what *rubris* means. I don't think it's a real word, actually. I know *rubric* has something to do with a purpose, but clearly the name of that ship was adapted.

"Do you know what happened aboard The Rubris?" Anther asks Rosie. "Are there any crewmembers aboard it? Are they safe for us?"

"I do not know," is all she says in reply.

All I know is that constantly ruminating about the meaning of *both* does the job of keeping my mind off the presence of that horrifying thing roaming freely somewhere aboard The Origin.

Rosie finally slows, and we gradually come to a halt behind her. "Here," she says, "it's time to stop and get some rest and water. In this room, everyone. Quickly. In you go."

My heart is pounding, and beads of sweat are rolling down my temples onto my neck and into my uniform. I'm envious of the others in their rec outfits; they're doubtless not as hot as I am right now.

We follow her into an enclosed room that thankfully has air conditioning against the heat down here. As I pass under the door jamb I see a diminutive, reflective gold label adorning it. *Shielding.*

Peering inside, it looks like a mess hall for maintenance, even though there's only a single

Engineer here. There's a fridge, countertops with a stove, freezer, and even a bed and a terminal. It all presents as severely antiquated, and it's in disarray, as if someone has gone to great lengths to make this tiny escape as homely – and dated – as possible.

If I didn't know any better, I would think someone could actually live in here. It's practically like a tiny little apartment. I wonder how many lonely meals or sleeps Rosie has had here. If she even eats or sleeps at all. I also wonder what the heck she even does down here. I make a plan to sit with her and learn more about her. It seems she is well aware of what we're dealing with, and that knowledge could be a comfort – or cause for anxiety. I guess I'll find out. I do want to know what 'shielding' references, anyway.

Everyone files in and sits down, winded and worn, placing their backs to the wall. No one sits at the center table or takes the bed. Rosie closes and locks the door. We watch her as she proceeds over to the far left corner to the terminal, where she closely stares into the screen and studies the data before her. I can only surmise she's tapping into Phiria to determine what happened. "Talicus, would you join me, please?"

The synthetic moves over beside her.

"Look at this," Rosie says, pointing to the screen. We're all too far away from the screen to see what she's showing Talicus, but I can see motion, and can just make out some movement through it, showing up in what appears to be monochromatic, night-vision-like footage. There is no sound.

"Fascinating," Talicus breathes.

"Hardly the word I would use to describe it," Rosie says. "But yes, there it is. God help us."

It's then that I realize they're watching footage from up above. I get up and start to make my way over to them. Rosie is instantly aware of me and turns toward me, both palms out. "No, Jax! Don't look. You mustn't look. That won't help you. None of you. Please sit down."

With surprising speed she whirls back around, and, with the flick of a key, the footage window is closed, and the screen darkens.

Talicus takes a deep breath and turns, standing lost in cybernetic thought.

Rosie rotates back to me once more. I just stand there, and we're face to face. "Are we safe in here, Rosie?" I ask her.

Rosie slowly nods. "For the time being." She looks around, as if appraising the room once more. "This is a radiation-proof room. In the event of any kind of meltdown or cataclysm aboard The Origin, this is one of the safest places you can be."

That makes sense. Thus, *Shielding*. Of course there would be a bed, fridge, freezer, and a way to keep tabs on the rest of the ship from here. This is where you would ride out the storm of a radiation leak, and hope against hope for the integrity of the room's seals to hold.

Orin chuckles grimly. "Cataclysm? Yeah. I'd say that's an appropriate word right about now." No one else laughs. Miritia lays her head on his shoulder. Orin puts his arm around her in comfort.

"Here we are, yet again, waiting," Donetis says despondently. "Where else can we even go on this ship? Rosie, is that thing coming?"

Rosie's eyebrows raise. She stands facing Donetis, hands clasped at her midsection. "I do not know, child. That's the truth. It could be anywhere. All we can do is try to track its whereabouts. Drink some water, children. We're allowed a little rest now, in a relatively safe space that's fairly soundproof from the outside. Take some comfort in that, and refresh yourselves."

And then it hits me in a sudden wave of suspicion.

Track its whereabouts.

How the heck did she just watch footage if the surveillance has been disabled?

"Rosie, Talicus disabled the surveillance. How were you able to even see what you just saw?" I ask.

"The lab is never disabled," she replies. "That's the one place on this ship that surveillance cannot be interrupted. The Phoenix Experiments exist because of this ship, and this ship exists because of the Phoenix Experiments. It's The Origin's sole purpose. It's the one place where there must always be a record. Additionally, the occupants of this ship are minors, and the Phoenix Experiments are medical. It's for your protection, and for the integrity of everything that goes on aboard this vessel."

"So, did you see when that thing entered our world, then? Is that what you saw?"

"Yes," she says, sadly. "That is what Baryonnis and I just saw, unfortunately." She sighs, and sits at the center table, facing most of us. The rest of us have to settle for her profile.

There's a lull; a wicked and overlong lull: I can hear our wheels turning, wondering what it looks like, what it can do, why it's here, and why on Earth Cryptus would go to such lengths to usher in something so demonic into our midst. Especially through an innocent little girl!

"Rosie," I pipe up, "can I ask you a question?"

She looks at me.

"You said you were… *dead*… before. You didn't mean, like… *dead* dead, did you?"

All of us wait with bated breath.

"It's a very long story, kiddo," she says to me. "I'm not sure a story of my death would interest you."

Hardly likely, lady, I think to myself.

"It would," I persist. "And I think it would interest all of us. Besides, you basically just confirmed it. Anyway, we all spend our days hooked up to a machine communing with the dead in long sessions, and we've been here a long time, suffering from deathly boredom. I'd say we're all well-acquainted with death and boredom to stomach it."

Rosie relents with a stubborn sigh. "Fine, fine. I was born in 1964. And… I died in 2045. I had just turned eighty-one years old when my number was up."

She smiles thinly.

I watch her, but frankly, I simply don't know what to say. 2045. That's 426 years ago. Rosie is technically, accounting for her two lives, 507 years old. The very notion blows me away.

But there's another notion. The bizarre idea that she might be a raving lunatic flashes through my mind, briefly. However, don't we deal with the paranormal aboard this ship anyway? We always have. And anyway, isn't that the point of the Phoenix Experiment to commune with those whom we've lost, and to even try to bring them back? My mind wonders, *who loved Rosie enough to bring her back?* Someone had to.

No one says anything. I'm sure everyone else is as uncertain what to say as I am. Rosie scans the room, reading our expressions.

"I know what you're thinking. I'm either crazy, or the Phoenix Experiments actually work. I'm not an illusion; I sit here before you a real, whole, alive-and-well human being, long past her prime. I've been 'there and back again,' as it were. And here I am before you today."

Talicus has been quiet and still, but now she's studying our elderly, resurrected companion, and she speaks up. "Facial and retinal scans confirm your identity. She is not lying, children. This is Rosalita Dahlia Campion, born December 8th, 1964, emigrated from San Juan Ixcoy, Guatemala to Matamoros, Mexico in April of 1985. Married to Miguel Monzon in August of 2034, longtime resident of Clarksville, Tennessee, and finally Washington, DC. Credentials include former spiritual adviser to the 49th President of the United States, Vance Brennan Cardona. You were there during the gorgon invasion of 2026 and the wars of the 40's following. And… deceased as of February 13th, 2045.

"You are who you say you are," Talicus ends.

I'm shell-shocked. If this woman truly was on the other side, and she's familiar with The Djinn, maybe she also knows how to defeat it.

"Your memory banks are overflowing with truth, Baryonnis," Rosie says, smiling gently. "And now my own memory banks are overflowing with emotion." Her eyes appear to fill as she is lost in thought, reflecting back over her lives… both of them. "You're perhaps looking at a living legend," she finishes, humbly.

"Incredible, Rosie," I gasp. "You were on the other side, and, now… you're back. What was it *like* there? How long were you dead- I mean, gone? And… what was it like when you were brought back? Did you see The Djinn there? I have so many questions!"

"That makes two of us," Anther echoes.

"Three," Omnias chimes in.

"Nope. Four," Alaris sounds off. I look over at her and smile, gently.

I watch as Rosie looks around the room and is met with sheepish nods as the others chime in as well, signifying they, too, want answers. It's time for her to indulge us all. For if she truly comes from the other side, then perhaps our parents can as well.

In the dark, sheltered corner of our vast ship, Rosie clears her throat. "Fine. This may surprise some of you. It won't be easy, mind you, but it will be the truth."

"It was peaceful. Like, being asleep," Rosie says. "I suppose you all have some experience with that, whether you're in actual REM sleep, or you've been wired up to those machines up there with your android hovering over you, watching from his booth."

Talicus has fetched water and doled it out to all of us. I look up at her and smile, thankful for her custodial prowess. I'm becoming more and more at home with her, despite the freshness of the horrible memory at the hands of her colleague. She is gentle, forthright, humble, and helpful, and maybe some of these AnthroMetas are in fact redeemable, I think. Time will tell, but for now, our new synthetic is on a roll. We drink and listen to Rosie.

"When I died, I saw what so many have reported. A bright light. It was both brief and interminable. Alarming and calm. Your emotions don't leave you; they carry through with you to the other side. But grief becomes assuaged, and it certainly did for me. When I left my husband and this world, I felt something dark and ominous was coming, but it was no longer my right or privilege to counsel those left behind through it. It was their own soil to till. The Father was calling me home, so, home I went. But, in the blink of an eye, I felt suspended on a time and plane that was the best of both worlds. Happiness, contentment, memories, fulfillment, tears of joy… all of it blended together until my heart nearly burst. I can't really describe it except to say that I felt *utterly* whole. I saw my mother, my Miguel eventually showed up, I saw those I had served with down here, family and good friends, my mother, father, dear Wyatt, his brother Cameron, Vance, I saw my children, Vance's wife Andi, and so many more. It was heartfelt and beautiful."

I have no idea who these people are, but they are precious to her. As she speaks, her cheeks bloom outward and her eyes light up, twinkling in memory of all those loved ones she reconnected with. I could practically feel the familiar joy heartthrob, the thrum of pure elation in seeing my own parents in my most recent Phoenix Experiment before Cryptus evicted me.

"Oh, I could still see you down here. Well, not *you* – this was well before your time, but wars came and went. Tyrants rose and fell. Oppressed peoples fought back, other invaders terrorize our world. We rejoiced with those who rejoiced, and we mourned with those who mourned, constantly praying for you.

"Earth has been woven through an endless tapestry of victories and defeats, joys and pains, laughter and tears through *many* centuries since I was called home."

But then Rosie pauses, and her smile dies. Her face grows careworn and tired. "I don't know when, but something eventually began calling me back. I don't know how long it was, nor why. I wanted to stay, you see. The Father had called me home, so why was I now being pulled back? I couldn't answer it, and no answers were given. Sometimes that is the way of things. But I cannot explain what it felt like other than to say that it was like a visceral tearing. Being pulled tautly by two distinct forces: one keeping me here, and one desperately tugging me back. If you've ever tried to run against gale force winds, that might describe it. I could not do it."

She stops and looks at me as she speaks her last words: "The winds eventually took me."

A coldness begins creeping over my heart just then, and I clutch my uniform closer to me. My breath begins to materialize in front of me a bit, and it feels as though the room has chilled from the air conditioning. I glance around. Others also clutch their clothing to themselves and sidle up beside their neighbors for added warmth.

"On my way back, I passed something. Time seemed to stretch; *everything* seemed to stretch as I felt pulled back through this brilliant vortex, light streaming around me. I was almost through, when I saw it. At first, it was beautiful, as all evil things are at first glance. It's only when you study them up close that you find they are full of malice and a staunchly evil will.

"It was *The Djinn*, children. Swirling around with me, it was seeking a way out. It reached for me. It clutched at me. Swirling smoke and fire encircled it, wreathed around it like amber scarves, twisting and flailing in the wind. You cannot make out anything but its eyes. They smolder with hate. Nothing has ever so filled me with raw horror on that side. It wanted me, but it could not grasp onto the intangible. That is what we both were, still, until I was pulled through, back here, to the other side. I awoke and clutched myself, wondering if it had come as well, through me. That's when I realized I was naked.

"Someone was in the room with me, in that lab. I only just caught a faint glimpse of them fleeing. I never found out who it was. I gathered what clothing I could find, jumpsuits like this one, covered myself, and fled to the lower levels. I was alarmed beyond belief, frightened, and lonely. I had no idea where I was, I had no idea why I was here nor what year it was; all I knew is that I wanted to get far, far away from that lab, and that place and that… presence."

I swallow, hard, as I listen to her.

Every mention of The Djinn fills me with unease, and I am still cold.

"Well," Rosie says – and I can tell she's finishing her story and bringing us to the present – "I finally found my way down here through the same vents and shafts young Anther has become so adept at traversing. There was no one else here. I thought I was going crazy, talking to myself, hearing voices, almost like intermittent poetry in my head…" -here I stop, flinching at what she has just said, and wondering if she's hearing the same orations I've been hearing- "a person could really go crazy down here.

"It was only through repeated trial and error that I found my way down here to this little, hovel, I guess you would call it, this 'safe room' as it were, and right there" -here she points with a gnarled finger over to the terminal she and Talicus were just at- "is where I learned all about you, the Phoenix Experiments, the Origin, the Zephyr, the Rubris, your chiefs, the year, the circumstances we were in, the banshees, the synthetics, and, finally… The Djinn. I discovered that's what it was that I had passed on my way back."

"You found out about The Djinn from that?" Orin asks her, pointing at the terminal.

"No," Rosie says. "That is not public record. If it were in there, Baryonnis would know about it as well. Earth would know about it. The other ships would have known. Someone would have stopped this entire process long before you came to me." She shakes her head. "No, it's just that young Anther here isn't the only one who used to crawl around shafts and eavesdrop." Anther grins at her once more. "I found out by eavesdropping. A conversation Stygius Cryptus was having – with *himself*. It was only recently. I spent many years searching this ship and trying to figure out where I had come from, who had brought me back, and what all of this was about. I couldn't just 'show up' on the main floors and say, 'Hi, I'm Rosie, I used to be dead but now I'm alive again, can you spare some BioPrime for a cold elderly Latina?" She laughs grimly. We chuckle in response. *"Ay caramba, mio Dios,"* she says, shaking her head once more, "this ship was never intended for its current purpose."

"What do you mean?" I ask her, growing ever colder. All of us continue to lean into her, regardless of time, the presence of The Djinn onboard The Origin, and our potential fate at the hands of either this spectral entity or Cryptus.

Rosie frowns and sighs. "Please understand, children, that The Origin doesn't need an Engineer. It never did. Neither did The Zephyr or The Rubris. These ships are self-sustaining. You know that. Modern marvels, you might call them. They are entirely reliant on their own programming, and they are solar-powered. They will not stop functioning unless destroyed, which is, alas, what befell The Zephyr through a freak accident."

Rosie stares me in the eye, and her lids narrow. "But it's what has happened down there that is far more important. In the throes of a death spiral, Earth had reached a point of no return. It can no longer sustain life to the same degree. Global warming, deforestation, alien occupation, madmen, ruthless tyrants, and more ensured that. The net effect has brought our beloved planet to its knees. Ergo, man devised a solution. They would find another world. So, they began to build ships. Great ships. Vast ships to carry us across the stars to a new home. Ships like the very one you're in. Like The Zephyr and The Rubris. These ships were supposed to house the last survivors of Planet Earth aboard them. Is it any surprise? They are *enormous*. They are not meant for just eight boys and eight girls and a few chiefs and synthetics. But… something went wrong. Something was unleashed down there. Something evil. It appeared one day from The Rubris, and then infiltrated our world."

"The banshees," little Dravin voices.

"Ohh, no…," Rosie says, looking at him with an endearing smile, "young Dravin, the banshees are a mere byproduct of The Djinn. They are of the same ethereal family. They are also evil, yes, but something *else* was unleashed, and it is the worst evil mankind has ever inflicted on itself."

We wait anxiously for her answer.

"The worst evil of mankind is mankind itself," she says, solemnly. "It always has been. Not gorgons nor black holes nor terrorism nor banshees nor The Djinn. No, children," she says, heaving a great sigh. "Mankind has always been the worst enemy of itself. And down there is where it all finally went wrong and fell apart. The banshees were sent in to clean it up."

"*Sent in?*" Orin cries, incredulous. "By whom?"

"Oh, the same person who has been playing this silly game with your lives and your consciences up here all this time, both awake and dreaming. Remember what I said about The Djinn: it can influence us, possess us, and cause mental illness. The Djinn has been doing so since the beginning of time. And it has been working overtime on one person in particular to thwart your progress."

In my heart, I already know who it is. "Stygius Cryptus," I say with a knowing grimace. I nod, the truth finally revealed to me in full.

But Rosie doesn't nod. She just stops me short and stares at me, shaking her head.

"No," she says. "It was none other than your helmsman. Fulsar Oculus."

What?!? nearly everyone exclaims except for Ranshay. His interpretation is somewhat delayed as Talicus processes all of this, but he does exclaim something unintelligible in Hindi. His eyes are wide. *Bilkul nahin! Tum mazaak kar rahe ho!* he cries.

"*Oculus* is behind this?" I, too, cry in dismay. "How? Why on earth would he let the banshees out, and… and… why would he bring you back? What is going *on* aboard this ship, for crying out loud? Are you saying that he let them all through, they got down to earth and started killing everyone, and so Cryptus killed him for it? That would be years ago now. Why would Cryptus wait all this time?"

"It's certainly conceivable," Talicus says.

I gaze at Rosie in incredulity.

"But that would make Cryptus and Mirabay the good guys!" I wail. "That just can't be!" I stare at her, almost pleading with her for a different logic; a better explanation.

"It most definitely can be, I assure you," Rosie says. "Helmsman Oculus let the banshees in, and now, something even more terrifying has now come through that poor little girl."

Then it hits me. "Wait – if Oculus let them through, he must have also let *you* through? Is that who did it? Why would he do that?"

"I honestly do not have an answer to either," she says, and that deflates me. "To my knowledge the Phoenix Experiments are meant to connect the loved to the beloved, the passed to the bereaved. Oculus and I are in no way related, I assure you. He would not love me – or know me – enough to want to bring me back."

Anther clears his throat. "This is what happened aboard the Rubris, isn't it, Rosie?"

She doesn't answer; she just clenches her lips tight and looks away. "We just don't understand the other side. It is beyond dangerous to toy with the eternal. The Rubris was banished for toying with this."

My head is spinning at all of these revelations. They are far too much information and bedtime ghost story to assimilate in one sitting. I also can't believe that Oculus is behind it, and that tears at me. I turn around and place my hands on my head. Alaris stands up and places her hand on my back in support. I turn to embrace her.

"I didn't say that it would be easy, people," Rosie concludes. "But I did promise to tell you the truth."

The truth is jarring. The truth is unacceptable. *The truth cannot be the truth.*

Rosie freezes momentarily, and her head bows. So does mine, simultaneously.

Earthen vessels, frail and weak
Thou shouldest hide, for the seek
    Is on at last;
    the beast is fast
Thy slow, thy lame, shall rot and reek

Malice eats it like a canker
It casheth chips as would a banker
    Start thy feet,
    beat thine retreat
Lest spirit quail 'midst stumping hanker

Rosie has told us what she has told us, and now I can see it in everyone's eyes: Fulsar Oculus, our own helmsman, was the enemy all along. But why would Cryptus flat out kill him? And why is he impersonating Oculus' voice up there? And why would Fulsar let the banshees through in the first place?

None of it makes sense, but it doesn't need to right now. The only thing that makes sense is bracing and panic, because we all hear it once more.

The Djinn.

Welling up from the depths of the ship, a mournful howl breaks out, and our flesh crawls. Alaris clutches me and moans, sinking into my uniform and burying her face. Rosie slowly turns toward the door.

The slow, agonized shriek is multi-noted with dissonant clashing pitches set against one another, designed to freeze the marrow and sap the lifeforce out of you. It grows horribly, and with it, our fear, as an unknown presence approaches outside the room we're holed up in. We can hear the dull throbbing growl fused with the cries of a thousand souls in agony intertwined in a cry that stops our hearts.

"Be… still," Rosie whispers. "Do *not* fear."

And then… it stops. We're met with silence, and the only sound is the overloud thud of our hearts in our ears, as an eerie spectral mist starts to seep under the doorway, slithering through the mists of the locked door seals.

As if waiting patiently for us to bolt, right outside, we hear nothing.

12: The Specter

No one says a word.

My eyes meet Alaris.' Hers are ringed with fear. I'm sure mine are as well.

All sixteen of us back away against the far wall. Only Rosie is left at the center of the room, standing there, silently, poised, steadfast and true, facing the door with grim determination.

Everything falls to a hush, and our hearts are in our ears. I can hear Anther swallow noisily from across the room. Omnias grips his hand so hard I think she'll break it. He flinches and looks down. "Ow."

His whispered utterance is far too loud.

The door to the room bursts open! The Djinn heard us! Fragments of heavy metal go spinning outward, ricocheting off the walls. One of them nails Skarbé in the head and chest, and then settles upon her, crushing her. She's instantly gone.

Sixteen of us left.

Cinders fly as burning fragments erupt around us and the wind grows thick with heat. It's hard to breathe!

A swirling, burning mist filters in amongst all of our desperate cries. Horrendous wind erupts around us as rushing trails of wavering corpse light stream around us, over us, under us and through us. I cannot contain my yells for help, but I have no idea who I'm calling for. Alaris tries to hide behind me.

Garris rushes toward it in a mad attempt to squeeze past it and out into the bowels of the ship, to dash off into the darkness. Where he thinks he'll go from there is anyone's guess.

It's useless.

The smoke literally seizes him; I watch with horror as a vice-like ethereal grip wraps around him and lifts him up in the air momentarily as his mouth drops and his eyes roll back in his head. He blackens from proximity to the heat of the beast. It screams at him: a wailing, ripping siren scream that sends fissures through every peace I've ever known. It holds him still while that high-pitched shriek drains every ounce of his lifeforce. Garris' face pales and his body goes limp. It tosses him violently against the far wall. He hits so hard he splats outward and then streaks down the wall to the floor. Garris is gone.

Fifteen.

Voices scream around me. Others try to avoid the smoke, but it just coalesces in front of them, gathering, gathering, gathering together, until it coils into an appendage-like mist, aiming for them. The screams never abate. Right now it's targeting Orin and Miritia, perhaps recognizing that he is the oldest and strongest of us youths. Both of them shield their face.

Where is Rosie? I wonder. I've lost her. In the hot, swirling vapor I can't see her.

Talicus shouts at it, but it merely roars at the synthetic nuisance and swipes her aside. She hits a side wall with a dull thud, collecting herself nearly immediately and standing stoic once more.

In the flickering darkness, there is not really silence. Like a whisper condemned, erased and forgotten; an abyss of empty air hungrily consuming memory and safety. The only thing that exists, then and there, is The Djinn.

Gaseous clouds of sizzling spectral light and shade swirl in a nebula of fear. My bones are scalded. I don't know where to go.

There's Rosie!

I see her now, amidst the swirling spray of blistering smoke streaming throughout the room. I cover my ears as the roaring scream resounds throughout this echo chamber, and my bones are chilled. She is eye to eye with The Djinn, if you can call it the thing's 'eye.' It's terrifying, catlike, and it sees all.

The thing screams at her, but she remains unafflicted.

"You have no power over me," Rosie says, calmly. "Get you gone, before your end comes for you."

The Djinn scowls and recoils, recognizing some power resident in this diminutive woman. It moves on. Instead, it targets those less stout; less sure of their place in this world; less emotionally stable.

Then the roar and scream combine into a spine-altering cacophony, and I can't take it. Alaris whimpers in fear beside me. I shut my eyes, but something draws near. The anguished cries of a thousand tormented souls are in that roar, as if it has feasted and grown fat on the dread of every one of its victims down through the ages.

The Djinn!

In the swirling, broiling mist, I can just make out the trails of smoke funneling toward me, their burning and grasping tentacles whipping and lashing. Without a sound I am suddenly engulfed, and Alaris' voice, crying out for me, suddenly sounds like a million miles away as it wraps around me.

I'm burning, yet intact. My head feels like it wants to explode. And then, I feel swallowed whole and devoured. Painless, yes, yet not without pain. It's almost like I'm disembodied and can see what's happening from a removed perspective. I hover observant and witness the silent, convulsing consumption of all that is me. Everyone scatters below as the bellowing smog hazes through all of us. Some of us run and make it out.

Donetis doesn't.

Ranshay doesn't.

Martos doesn't.

Ghirishia and Raelia don't.

They are plucked from their positions, elevated into the air, and forced to face The Djinn. There is a face in that smoke, and it is utterly evil yet familiar – where have I seen that face before? With a scream that is part raspy intake of breath and part exhale of soul-numbing anxiety, it sucks their very lifeforce out of them. Their eyes turn a ghostly, pallid white and recede inside blackened sockets of a death mask. Their faces go sallow like shriveled raisins, devoid of essence, and their fleshly shells fall limply to the ground, flaming, and do not rise again.

They burn to cinders.

Ten left.

Calmly brutal, brutally calm, the wraithlike beast devours me into its otherworldly self. I am forcibly yanked and ripped away from Alaris as she curls into a fevered fetal ball, horrified and tremulous

as I am wrenched away. And then I hear it, louder
than ever before as pangs of alarm buffet my body on
every side:

> *The time is now to make one's stand*
> *For ghostly terrors stalk the land*
> > *Abating not,*
> > *the hard fight fought*
> *They seeketh recompense from man*

> *And thou art chosen, humble boy*
> *From rank and file, pride and joy*
> > *They careth never*
> > *whithersoever*
> *Fleeth thee; thou art their ploy*

Sanity leaves me as I scream for my life and
am pitched into the wind of this roaring, scalding
phantom. I can see myself engulfed by it, and then I
blow away into a million pieces: fragmented, like
chaff. The screaming wind punctures me like a million
needles, seeking a way inside me, lusting for my
lifeforce, yet thwarted in taking it. I can't explain it; I
clutch myself and find that I'm still intact, whipping
around in the roaring wind.

And then, suddenly, I hear other voices.
Indistinct, I can barely pick them apart, but they are
male and female. Calling, shouting, railing against
The Djinn, they come, and I can feel The Djinn shiver
with me inside it. The smoke convulses, wavering and

blowing about the room, untethering from itself and desperately maneuvering and rejoining to stay intact; blowing, blowing, flickering and shaky, wisping and deftly regathering. And then, finally, with an awful cry of revulsion and defeat, it screeches into a chilling hiss and vanishes, dissipating into nothing.

A brilliant flash of fiery light erupts all around us, accompanying a deathly screech from monstrous vocal cords retreating further into the ship.

The Djinn is gone.

I fall to the floor and hit my head. Rosie runs to me and tends to me as the wisps of smoke dissipate into nothing and retreat. Talicus fetches a fire extinguisher and goes to work.

My heart is pounding, my eyes are bleary with tears, and my head is swimming and drenched in ethereal sweat or some kind of vaporous, steaming moisture.

The survivors are all coughing. But not all of us are survivors; some are quiet and lay still.

Bodies litter the floor. Just like that, seven of us are deceased. And now I have no idea if it's eight, because I now know that that evil face in the smoke belonged to little Zaris, and at last I believe she's dead.

"Alaris?" I cry. "Alaris!"

"I'm here, I'm here, Jax. Oh my gosh, are you okay?" She runs to me and hugs me. I fall into her embrace, weak-kneed and trembling. I can see Rosie over her shoulder, standing there, looking winded. I don't know what kind of battle this woman has just fought, but her body and face bear the marks of tortuous exertion and fatigue. Somehow, she manages to smile at me.

But then I don't see it. I see something else.
Just a flicker…
I can't make it out.

I slowly pull myself away from Alaris, and she looks at me, confused. Rosie sees my eyes fixed at a point beyond her, and she turns to examine what I'm fixated on.

And then, she turns back to me and smiles.

But it's all I can do to keep from crying.

There, standing in flickering, spectral light, illuminated faintly by their own lifeforce, stand a man and a woman. They are not completely formed; their bodies fade into translucence at wavering points, obscured and then solid again. They linger on the edge of life and death and wait for me.

I know them! I know them well. In every single dream I've had aboard this wretched ship since the day I lost them, I've sought them, sought to be held by them, to hold them one last time and hear them tell me that they have loved me every single day we've been apart.

To hear them say they're proud of me.

My eyes fill with tears as I stumble toward them. Unaware of my own limbs, I reach out for them, fingers snapping in reflexes I can't control.

They're here. Both of them.

My parents, taken from me.

Mom and Dad.

They smile gently, and stand there as we regard each other. I cannot hold them, this I know, but perhaps, for a few precious moments in time, we can commune, and I can tell them that I've missed them with everything that is in me, as my heart swells to a capacity near bursting with yearning.

We just smile at each other in recognition.

No one says a word.

13: The Found

———

I cannot believe my watery eyes.

I draw near to them, while their shimmering apparitions hold steady. They are in tears, and so am I. As I pass Rosie, she whispers four words only.

Go to them, Jax.

I don't even look at her; I only have eyes for my parents.

I stand before them, and they look me over.

Their voices ring through to this world loud and clear, though I'm well aware that there is a great spiritual gulf between us.

"Son, we've missed you so much," says my Mom amidst tears.

"You look so tall," says my Dad.

"You look *brave*," says my Mom once more.

"Mom, Dad...I-I saw you," I stutter, sniffing, "I saw you the other day in the Phoenix Experiment."

"We know, Jax. We wanted to-" my Mom starts, but her lip quivers. An invisible light from the other side catches a shimmering tear dripping down her ghostly cheek. "We so wanted to come through with you. To tell you. To *warn* you. But it just wasn't in the cards for us. I'm so sorry, my son," she says in practically a whisper.

My own lip is quivering, and the tears are bathing my cheeks. An arm drapes over my shoulder as Alaris draws near. She stands next to me, to my right. I want to glance over at her, but I fear a *blink-and-you'll-miss-it* moment where the connection is severed, and my parents vanish. But it does beg a question.

"How are you even here?" I ask. "How can you be here without coming through the chamber in the lab? Can you stay? *Will* you stay?" I ask, and it sounds like pleading. I'm okay with it. I don't even care about the answers... I just want them here.

I just want them with me.

I just want them to stay... forever.

I'm dimly aware of a presence on my left now. I can tell it's Anther. He's also crying with me. By now, we've shared plenty of stories of how painful it's been not to reconnect with my parents in the Phoenix Experiments.

My heart is in my throat.

"We're in The Transference," my Mom says. "It won't last long. The Djinn came through, and we rode that wave in to you, but it's fading, Jax. Every wave that washes along the shore must recede. It pulls at us even now."

"I miss you *so* much, Mom and Dad," I say, and now I'm bawling. "I've- I've tried to live up to what I thought you wanted for me, who you hoped for me to be. I-"

It's no use. I can't complete that sentence, and I hold my palms out and upward in futility. Rosie shifts and slightly gasps behind me.

"Son, we love you. We're proud of you, kiddo. You needn't worry about us. There are far greater things to worry about right now," my Dad says, and my eyes are drawn to him. A shimmering translucence takes them momentarily, and their images quietly flicker. I reach for them as my jaw drops.

"Jax, listen," my Dad whispers, urging me, "there's no time. You can still bring us through, but you *must* get to the lab to do so. There's no other way. The Djinn *must* be stopped, Jax."

"They must be stopped at all costs," my Mom adds. "We know the secret, Jax. We hold the key.

But we must come through; we must be *there* – on the other side – in order to stop them."

I sniff, gathering focus and strength into my will just as I gather air into my lungs. I nod quickly.

They quickly fade once more, the light flickering around them as, momentarily, I see right through them.

"Jax," my Mom says, reaching for me. I mirror her, and our fingers pass through each other in yearning, feigning physical connection. "If we don't make it through, if we…," she trails off. A pleading smile clenches her lips. "Always know that we love-"

They fade from view suddenly, abruptly. My heart lurches.

They're gone.

Again, just like that hot and cruel day, August 16th, 2466, they are taken from me once again, and I am reduced to bawling, consoled in the embrace of my friends. Elderly arms wrap around me, and a bespectacled gray-headed woman bows her temples against me as I quake with sadness for those I've lost.

And found.

And lost once more.

And found.

And lost yet again.

We don't know where The Djinn went, but we are allowed a moment's peace, because there's something important we have to do. Something awful.

It's time to tend to the dead.

We gather the scorched body of Dravin Mosopathen, only 8 years old, the youngest of us here, who loved to draw. His face is frozen in horror, seized forever in the throes of deep emotional shock.

All of theirs are.

We gather the charred body of Ranshay Filipath, 12 years old, who never knew a lick of English and probably never knew what hit him.

We gather the seared body of the big oaf, Garris Granthis, 15 years old, who showed bravery trying to show us the way of escape.

We gather the blackened body of Martos Mixtros, 16 years old, nevermore the life of the party. As in life, his energy died out long before its time.

We gather the body of Skarbé Bognis, 15.

We gather the body of Donetis Tarnie, 16.

We gather the body of Raelia Forgrim, 13.

All of them, killed by The Djinn.

The best we can do is lay them together across Rosie's bed here in this horrible room, *Shielding,* hoping against hope that their bodies will be shielded. We drape the sheets across their bodies in reverence, and then stand quietly before them.

Alaris sighs, staring at her dead friends. "I wonder what their parents feel now, rejoined with them. This irony is wicked," she groans. "They worked so hard at controlling their emotions to bring their parents into life back *here*, and yet The Djinn scared their emotions right out of them here and sent them to their parents in death *there*."

I feel the wicked irony too. "Our whole purpose on these ships was to bring them back." I shake my head. "At least they're together again."

Rosie doesn't answer. Instead, she offers a prayer, and speaks a quiet Mexican blessing over their bodies. I don't know what it means. But then I understand why Rosie gasped behind me when I put my palms out in front of my parents.

She does the same thing now, holding her palms up and glancing over at me, solemnly. A heartfelt smile slowly spreads across her face.

"This, Jax," she says, "is receiving. We receive whatever comes our way, knowing that The Father loves us and will eventually work it out for our good. I've done this for five centuries now. I will never stop doing it, because I will never stop receiving what The Father allows in my life, knowing that His will for me is good. I hope the same is true for you," she then concludes, smiling once more. I nod to her.

Maybe we're supposed to receive wicked irony from The Father as well, I think.

"It's time to be numb, children," Rosie says, finishing. "The Djinn – and the banshees – thrive on emotion. They thrive on pain, rage and fear. We must be bold, of staunch will, and resolute."

Rosie walks over to me and stands before me.

"Jax, your parents are correct. You must reconnect with them, and The Djinn must be stopped."

We're on the move again. We can't stay here. By now we're heading back upward, and though it's unstated, we all know what I have to do. I must get to the Phoenix lab and focus all my energy on bringing my parents through.

I *must*.

All things hingeth now on this,
So carefully thread thou paths amiss
They wayward not,
are danger-fraught
To revelations not of bliss

Harken not to voice of angst
Pleadeth it shall, with no thanks
Be thou wise,
open thine eyes
Lest passion cheat thee from thy ranks

I'm confused by this one, and wonder if Rosie has heard the same thing and is equally perplexed, but we must move on. These poetic whispers do little to portend or forecast; but I trust that they come from a voice that bridges the gulf between the past and the future; otherwise, why would I even hear them? Someone, somewhere, has made sense of them, I trust. Maybe that someone will eventually be me.

We're moving away from the engines, up and up, back toward the lab. *This is it.*

At some point we happen upon an observation window into a massive room we hadn't passed by before. Peering inside, there are thousands upon thousands of chairs for a vast audience. It's then that I realize Rosie was right. This ship was meant to hold all of the survivors, not just us. *Everyone.*

The truth barrels into me. It was never meant to be this way. We've all been lied to.

I cannot believe my eyes.

14: The Showdown

There's no turning back now.

Talicus continues to offer direction and leadership, folding in right alongside Rosie. They've conversed and planned, and have now decided to take us away from the *Shielding* room, as that was both the location of the attack, as well as our last known coordinates. We don't want The Djinn *and* Cryptus on our tail.

In ten minutes, we'll reach a point, they say, where we'll ultimately have to diverge; a few of us will go with me as protection against Cryptus, Mirabay and the others, and the rest will hide.

Talicus recommends that she and Orin, being the strongest of us, come with me to the lab and help me summon my parents; Anther may come as well. The rest will stay with Rosie. Talicus has conducted the exact same Phoenix Experiments aboard The Zephyr. She'll know how to get me in there and then it's up to me to try to bring them through. *And*, I think with a shudder, *she's strong enough to take on Cryptus… hopefully.*

So, it's decided.

"Is surveillance still down?" Venthix asks.

"Yes," Talicus confirms.

"What about the Achilles? What's their ETA?" asks Orin, walking somberly alongside Miritia.

"ETA 48 minutes, Finorin," she replies.

"*Orin,*" he corrects her.

"Fine. Orin," she confirms. "I'm in touch with the Achilles' central computer. Commander Krux is aboard, with a team of twenty-one. They're aware of our situation."

"Including the attack just now?" I ask.

"Yes."

"I hope they don't turn away," I add, glumly. "What can they even do? Do they have weapons?"

"Yes," Talicus confirms.

That's some comfort, I think.

But then I click my tongue. "Why did I even ask that? They won't be of any use against The Djinn, of course."

"Jax, their weapons are not for use against The Djinn," Talicus replies, and she looks at me coldly. "They're to restore order and take Cryptus, Mirabay, and possibly the chiefs, into custody."

I nod, solemnly, pondering the prospect of a firefight aboard The Origin. I don't know if there are any weapons aboard our ship, or if Cryptus and Mirabay have armed themselves. But it may just come down to that.

"We will remain in hiding. Cryptus and Mirabay won't know where we are, but I've established a secure channel with the Achilles. Once they dock, Commander Krux – and Commander Krux only – will be relayed our location securely."

"And we have no idea on the status of our chiefs?" I ask. "If they're alive, held captive, anything?"

Talicus shakes her head. "I find no record of their status in Phiria. Apparently, Cryptus has taken the liberty of purging their data. We won't know until, or *if*, we actually happen upon them."

I shake my head once more. "That's four strong, grown adults we could definitely use right now. I wish we knew."

"I do as well, Jax," says Talicus.

"48 minutes," breathes Venthix. "*Man.* A lot can happen in that time. Whatever we can do to speed things up and get this over with, so much the better. I do *not* wanna see that thing again.”

“Me neither,” Omnias growls. “Not ever again. Did any of you see the face in-”

“No!” Rosie exclaims, whirling back around to Omnias. “Don’t say it. Whatever you saw, keep to yourself, young Omnias. It is for your eyes only, not for quaking hearts in the dark.”

My heart is quaking, and I’m in the dark. All our hearts are quaking, and we’re all in the dark.

And I know exactly what Omnias saw.

It was Zaris.

At last, after trudging on for our ten minutes, mostly back uphill, we reach the divergence point.

“Here we are,” Rosie says nonchalantly, and she sighs, tapping some conduits running alongside the wall as she turns to us. She’s not very winded or sweaty; the woman has been reinvigorated from her reincarnation, and she looks healthy and strong.

The throbbing of the ship has lessened as we’ve climbed, and it still punches through the air around us, but less so than that horrid thing we just encountered.

“Now, it’s time to split up. Talicus, Orin and Anther will go with Jax. I will take Venthix and the four girls here.”

"Three," Alaris says. Rosie cocks an eyebrow and tilts her head. "*Three,*" she repeats. "I'm going with Talicus and Jax."

"Young Alaris, I hardly think this is the time to-"

"I'm going with them," Alaris says defiantly, "or I'm waiting right here until the end."

No one says anything. Rosie relents. "Fine, child. Just remember, Jax is the priority. He must bring his parents through. That's all that matters up there. Protect him at all costs," she says to Talicus, Orin, and Anther.

"No funny business. Be a *gent,*" Anther cautions Venthix, pointing at him. Venthix will be alone with the three girls and Rosie.

Venthix smirks. "I will. Be careful."

Omnias and Anther slowly separate, their hands still clasped, as she retreats toward Rosie. Suddenly, Anther whips her back to himself and kisses her hard. Everyone snickers.

Orin glances at Miritia. "Aw, hell. Me too," he says, and then he does the same with Miritia.

Ghirisha stands alone, blushing. For a moment, she looks sheepishly at Venthix. He smiles nervously at her, and shrugs. She smiles appreciatively at him, knowing they'll be together, and he takes her hand.

"Alright, children, now that we've said our goodbyes, can we get a move on?" Rosie chirps with a slightly remonstrative affect. "It's already hot enough down here in this ship without you adding to it."

More giggles.

"Be careful, Rosie," Talicus says. "Take cover and wait for my signal. I'll have Phiria make the announcement when the time comes and we're all clear. We'll proceed to the lab and prepare the Phoenix Experiment for Jax." Rosie nods.

"What happens when we get to the lab? Can we lock it so that they can't get inside?" I ask.

"Certainly, unless Cryptus has changed the access codes," Talicus responds.

"Can he do that?" Anther says.

"Most definitely," says our synthetic.

"But you won't know until we get there," I say.

"I won't. There is only one way to find out."

We gather our courage, sighing heavily. "Well, let's get up there." There's only forty-plus minutes until the Achilles arrives, and we don't want The Djinn roaming around this ship when they come. "Let's go get my parents," I say, decisively.

Anther nods at me, his jaw clenched.

Orin chimes in. "Let's do this."

"Never forget," Rosie cautions us as we eye each other across the dividing line of our teams, "The Djinn wants you to feel. You must not give it any emotion. You must *not* give it any fear. Stuff your emotions way down, children. Seal them off, or The Djinn will have you."

They regard her somberly.

Talicus breaks the silence. "Rosie, Jax, let us consult for a moment. The rest of you may disperse. I have an idea, and I'd like to discuss it with the two of you privately, if you don't mind. Phiria has been compiling data, and I've been searching through it. Something has just come to light, and I humbly request your feedback."

Rosie and I agree, and we're deep in counsel for a bit. What I hear has bearings on all of us.

"Are you okay?" Alaris asks me, once we break. She can tell that something's up.

"Yes. I'm fine," I say, wiping the tears from my eyes. I'm lying of course, but what more can I do? "Let's get moving. I'm okay. We can talk in a bit."

She relents, and Anther leads the way this time. Talicus is right behind him, should we run into any unexpected interference from Cryptus or any of the others.

I ask for an ETA on the Achilles. Our android reports they're 33 minutes from docking. They know to come in armed and brandishing weapons, Talicus informs us. At this I shake my head, and my eyes widen in incredulity that it's all come to this. I hope against hope that there's no weapons fire exchanged aboard The Origin. Everyone knows: one bad shot and we can all enjoy a healthy dose of depressurization as we're sucked out into space and are frozen.

But maybe it's better to freeze in the grip of space than burn to death in the fist of The Djinn.

We creep along, quietly, Anther leading the way. There's no sign of anyone, but there are muted sounds at various intervals: sounds of someone talking throughout the ship. A large din erupts at one point to our right, far outside the shaft that we're in, which propels us onward and sends trembling fright through our midst. Ultimately, it's not that which we all fear.

The Djinn.

I wonder where it is aboard our ship… where it went after the attack that killed our friends… where it will strike next. My thoughts go to Rosie and Alaris, Venthix and the others, and I pray quietly for their safety.

It's a long haul.

We trudge on, quietly, for perhaps another ten minutes or so. I see the signs that we've now entered Quadrant C, and I think we're still a few floors down from Subfloor 3A. Cryptus' lab has to be somewhere around here, but I trust Anther knows where he's going. After all, this is where we got in trouble with Cryptus. If that event isn't seared into his memory, I don't know what is.

We creep along, as quiet as mice now.

Quadrant C, Subfloor 3A, Room 319.

Finally, we're here. Talicus takes the lead and turns around to us, putting her finger to her lips. We're at the maintenance shaft outside the lab: the very one Cryptus caught Anther and I outside those years ago.

The incident with the blue pen.

Anther and I were so little then. Younger than Ranshay, to be sure, but not nearly as young as little Dravin. *Poor Dravin,* I think, shaking my head. That little boy. I trust he's reconnected with his parents. Ranshay too. And Garris, Martos, and the girls from The Zephyr. I never want to see The Djinn again.

Orin grabs a metal pipe he's found lying in the shaft, and from the looks of it he plans to use it as some kind of weapon in our attempt to seize control of the lab. I momentarily regret not having anything of my own to wield, but then realize that our greatest weapon is Talicus herself.

"Alright, here is the plan," says our synthetic. "You'll follow me out. I'll take the lead. If Cryptus is in the lab, that will make it harder, but I will attempt to subdue him. You'll follow me in and lock the lab door behind you. It will be secure *and* soundproof from the outside. No one will know we're in there. I will program in a new code for Phiria to disable the lock. Jax, you can then hop onto the bed and the others can get you wired up for the Phoenix Experiment. I've already confirmed with Phiria that it's live. It's been live and running since The Djinn came through, so you won't have to fire up anything. Once you're on the bed, I will send you in, and the others can stand guard. Got it?"

We all nod.

"Okay, time to go. Watch out, Anther, please," she says. Anther moves aside. Talicus then literally opens the tip of her finger, folding it back to reveal a long and periscoping Phillips head. She slowly inserts it with precision into the four mounting screws on all sides of the vent shaft. Her finger-screwdriver emits only the slightest whirring noise.

She then undoes the locking clasps. Talicus is utterly surgical and silent in her work, as she finally removes the vent shaft grate.

We filter out, slowly, Talicus in the lead. Orin follows her, and then Alaris, me, and then Anther at the rear. He replaces the grate over the aperture we've just emerged through, and then follows us.

Talicus motions for us to wait as she approaches the corner in the corridor leading to 3A. There are no sounds except the distant drumming of the ship, and the occasional sounds of voices murmuring from some far-off point.

We're outside the lab now.

Talicus leans around the corner and peers into the Phoenix lab. She jerks back suddenly, bracing herself against the wall. Her expression does not change; it's one of mathematical focus.

She presses herself against the wall, turns to us slowly, eyebrows up, and thumbs into the room, shaking her head. It's then that we realize someone is in there, and that it's most likely Cryptus. We'll have to do this the hard way.

A chill runs through me. *How could we be so stupid?* I think to myself. *Of* course *he's in there. Where else would he be?*

Our android motions for us to wait here. She gathers her programming, sticks out her chin, and suddenly, she's walking around the corner into the lobby of the Phoenix lab as if out on a leisurely stroll. We hear everything.

"Hello, Stygius Cryptus."

Movement. Sounds like Cryptus is now standing, facing her.

"Baryonnis Talicus. Where have you- I mean- where did you vanish to? We humbly requested for everyone to report to the Assembly Hall."

"I am aware of the directive. I was unable to comply. Someone had disabled my programming and I had entered sleep mode."

"Sleep mode? Who would even know how to do such a thing aboard The Origin? Those codes are proprietary to each synthetic, and coded to each ship. Yours are active only aboard The Zephyr, as are mine aboard only The Origin."

"Yes, I know. I cannot speculate who it was nor why; we were gathered in the rec hall when it happened."

"You've been powered down in the rec hall? We were in there and did not see you. How long?" Cryptus' voice and questions are laden with suspicion.

"I do not know. Someone was quick enough, but how or why, I do not know, Cryptus. Nonetheless, I would like to respectfully file an anomaly report."

"Of?"

"It might be easier if I show you. May I?"

"Certainly."

More movement. The guessed sounds of Talicus moving to Cryptus' console. This all sounds vaguely reminiscent of how Cryptus set Oculus up to kill him: this whole *it's better if I show you* approach.

Before we know it, there is a scuffle. I don't know who is besting who; all I know is that we need to get in there and close that outer door *now* so that no one hears us.

"Move, move!" I whisper, and we filter into the room, single file. Orin goes first, wielding his metal pipe. He's followed by me, and then Alaris, then Anther. Ant closes the door and locks it.

"Talicus!" Anther cries. "It's closed, do your thing, you efficient and effective synthetic!"

I see Talicus. Her eyes flutter. From behind me, the door beeps in response, and a whirring sound emits. It's locked and disabled, just as she said.

"Anther! *Jax!*" cries Cryptus. "What are you-"

My eyes are drawn to the viewing room where Cryptus is pinned down to his console with Talicus behind him. She isn't breathing hard and doesn't look the least bit exerted. Her strength is horrifying. Briefly I wonder what a punch in the chest from Talicus would have done to me.

Talicus has Cryptus in a headlock, and he is fighting to remain sentient. The same arteries that feed our brains oxygenated blood are mimicked within AnthroMeta bodies, and whatever fluid keeps his synthetic brain functional, that's what Talicus appears to be clamping down on and restricting flow through.

I run to the other side of the viewing window and stare at him. "Yeah, how do you like that, *punk?*" I ask, fanning out my arms. "Doesn't feel so nice, does it, you *murderer!*"

"Jax, let me expl-"

"Quiet!" Talicus orders. Cryptus cannot move; his right arm is pinned behind him, and Talicus has his headlock secure. Cryptus grimaces, pulling at her arm with his free hand. "Jax, start the sequence, please. We don't have time," she instructs coolly. "I've got this one."

Behind us, Talicus has also dimmed the outer window to Cryptus' foyer, so no one can see in.

We move into the lab. Just as we do, Talicus gasps and grunts, and we all whirl back around. Orin holds up his metal pipe in a reflex.

The two androids are fighting. It is a clash of the titans as we watch with widened eyes.

Talicus appears to have some sort of aluminum shaft jammed through her hand; the hand that Cryptus was gripping.

Cryptus shoves her, and she flies back against the wall. He advances toward her, suddenly, and her right leg flies up in response, nailing him in the chest.

He grimaces again, but they are utterly soundless in their combat, eyeing each other with cold disdain.

Talicus jumps and spins, sending another impressive sidekick into Cryptus' face. She is graceful and deft in her movement, and I'm reminded of the old Martial Artists of eons ago, and the movies made glorifying their mode of combat. She is obviously equipped with similar programming, though I don't know what branch it is, whether Karate, Judo, Jujitsu, Taekwondo, or something else that is formidable, deadly, and cybernetic. *Just glad it wasn't me that pissed her off,* I think to myself. *She would destroy me in a heartbeat.*

Cryptus hits the window and blanches, eyeing us for a moment as his face is literally propelled into the glass. He steadies himself, his fake fingers pressed up against the pane, his hot pseudo-breath fogging the thin sheet of glass separating us.

He turns back to Talicus with emotionless determination. Talicus comes at him with a double-punch, and he deftly dodges both, calculating, predicting, and evading.

He circles up and launches an uppercut in response. Talicus flies back against the wall, instantly shaking her head. She jerks erratically for a moment, and it seems like Cryptus scored a major hit.

He rushes at her and pins her against the wall, firing blow after blow into her staunch form. She recoils, but reaches out to steady herself against a side counter table.

Talicus grasps something. I don't know what it is. She conceals it against her form as Cryptus continues to pummel her over and over.

In a flash, Cryptus then reaches up and clutches her head, right hand reaching around toward the front, and left hand, inverted, palming the back. In a singular violent move, he jerks her head to the right, presumably severing cords and cabling inside her.

Talicus spasms. White flashes emit from her neck. She fires one last reflexive elbow into Cryptus' ribs, and he jumps backward, but he is still holding her, and will not let go. He grips her head ever tighter, his right arm wrapped around her neck, and his left hand reaching behind her head to grip her chin.

To our horror, we watch as he rips Talicus' head clean off. Alaris screams and covers her mouth. We all cover our mouths.

"No!" Anther shouts.

I'm speechless.

Talicus' body slumps, but doesn't collapse. It stands there, immobilized, shorting out, and sparking; her arms flinch, waving in front of her pointlessly.

Neither of them is breathing hard. Well, at least *Cryptus* isn't breathing hard.

"Cryptus, you murderous bastard!" Orin screams, and he makes a move toward him with his metal pipe. But then he stops, thinking better of it. He starts to yell something else, but closes his mouth.

Alaris grips his shirt and pulls him back.

"No! Orin, *no!*" she screams.

Cryptus, holding Talicus' severed head, glances back at us coldly through the window for a moment. "I would have preferred it not end this way," he says with zero disdain. It is a statement not out of revenge, but rather cold, calculating logic far beyond that of mortal man. Built on algorithms, computations and programming we'll never understand; he knows this.

Talicus is dead. She stands there, motionless, sparks flying from the nape of her neck.

Cryptus calmly places her head on the console by the window, facing us, perhaps to taunt us. He turns back to her dead form, grasping the aluminum shaft that he had previously stabbed clean through Talicus' hand.

He doesn't see her open her eyes or wink at us.

In a blinding flash, her headless body whips around with astonishing speed and smacks Cryptus with something hard and cylindrical. He loses his balance and falls back against the console, hands up in defense.

Talicus' head is knocked loose and sent flying to the floor. The rest of our android is upon him, smacking the aluminum shaft from his right hand with her left, and then she reveals what she had been clutching.

In one blinding flash, she brings the Stasis interrupt pod down upon his forehead, sending unwelcome voltage coursing through his circuitry. Cryptus pops and shivers, sparks and shudders, jerking and spasming. The android's movements slow, and he slowly slumps down below our line of visibility, under the console. A dim thud sounds, and he's on the floor.

Our decapitated android stands there, reconciling with his immobilized body, and then she sets the Stasis interrupt pod down on the counter. Talicus reaches down to the floor for something.

In a gruesome move, she holds her own head, regards it with invisible eyes, and then slowly places her own head upon her shoulders. With an icy whisper, she starts reciting programming codes, executable file numbers and system diagnostics.

A strange flesh-colored gel oozes out of the ripped seam of her neck, coalescing together and then running the circumference of her severed neck, filling the grisly seam Cryptus created in beheading her. Her head twitches, she rotates her pate slowly to the right and left, and then turns to face us, blinking.

"Jax, Orin, Alaris, Anther, good to see you in one piece. I am victorious. Indeed, Hell hath no fury like an android scorned."

We laugh nervously, nodding, relieved.

"Talicus! Nicely done!" I say to her between near-tears. "Whoo-hoo! You're amazing."

"I will be once again. I need to reboot, Jax, and reroute damaged circuits. Please, get ready. We haven't time. I'll be right back. I am forming a plan as we speak. I'll brief everyone here on it when I am fully power-cycled.

"Good luck, Jax!" Talicus says, and then her eyes grow dim. Her form slumps. She's offline.

We don't waste any time. I hop in the first bed, and Orin and Anther wire me up.

I have no idea where The Djinn is. I don't want to see it again. Alaris hovers over me as I lay there, preparing to relax and waiting for the white noise. "You going to be okay? You better be," I warn her, hollowly.

"I'll be fine. We have a beheaded android here, rebooting." She pauses, looking comically uncertain for a moment. "I *think* I'll be fine."

"Ha! Okay then. I'm glad. Just…," I falter.

Her nose crinkles as she frowns. "Just what?"

"Keep your eyes peeled. That thing is still somewhere on this ship. Be careful. Remember Rosie's words. *Stuff your emotions way down, children. Seal them off, or The Djinn will have you.*"

She nods. "I will. I promise. You be safe as well, okay?"

I nod and smile. And then she kisses me again.

This time, it's even better than the first. I stare deeply into her eyes as the white noise kicks in, and I start to drift off.

Alaris pulls away. The ring starts to spin over me. As I am drawn into the Phoenix Experiment, I hear Anther chuckling. "You guys…" I grin, and the last sight I see is Alaris staring down upon me with her gorgeous red hair draping her shoulders like fire.

Swiftly now, the venture goeth
Speeding breakneck as he knoweth

One aim only:
save the lonely
Though the deadly tension groweth

Where the beast now wanders free
Can the dangerous tide stemmed be?
Answers fleeting
bear repeating
And truth will out even if desperately

There is truly no turning back now.

15: The Revelations

The Phoenix Experiment is just never what you expect.

I'm in. It's warm here. I can smell the freshly cut grass, the light drops of dew on an August morning in the sunshine, and it smells whole and clean.

I hear the poetic voice… it echoes through my cranium like a dream as I wander.

"Mom! Dad!" I shout. I train myself to be cold. No emotion. Impervious and protected from The Djinn. If somehow, it's back in here, I've got to shut myself off, as Rosie says. Just like with the banshees, I've got to own my emotions and restrain them. I'm in charge, not them. *Me.*

I don't know how long I've been in, but it feels like it's been a good few hours. I'm not sure. Inside the Phoenix Experiments, time becomes immemorial and you lose all sense of the space-time continuum. It could be yesterday, for all I know. The only thing I'm certain of is it's August, because that's when my parents were killed, and that's usually where I end up.

"Mom? Dad?" I yell, searching. I don't know where I am at first, but then the neighborhood coalesces into a hazy clarity. It's scorched… less clear than the memories of Cryptus and Talicus' epic battle.

I turn around and see it.

My house. There it is again. Last time, I was exiting it, and they were coming toward me. Now, I'm approaching it.

But where are they?

Dimly, I see the front door opening up. Slowly, and dreamlike, light streams out. I peer through the mist…

…and there they are. Once more, appearing through a fog and smiling at me from out of a dream, there are my parents.

My parents!

There they are!

Nothing stops me from rushing at them this time, running straight into their arms. We collide in an embrace.

I can smell my mother. Her long, flowing hair. I can feel my father. His giant muscles and stout form. They hold me and press me tightly against them, as if vast tentacles were reaching out threateningly to pull us apart once more, and they are avowed to never again let me go. I know I feel the same.

For a split second I wonder how they are faring back there: Talicus, Orin, Anther… and Alaris. And then, from the recesses of my memory, Rosie comes to mind, Venthix… Omnias, Miritia, Ghirisha... I'm resigned to trust that they're all okay.

I can't wait to introduce all of them to my parents. I just can't wait! I'm seized by emotion and in the throes of utter fulfillment as they hold me. We're all weeping, and the tears flow from our eyes like a wine of blessedness to quench a parched soul.

My Mom suddenly laughs. Her laughter rings out like mirth, unburdened by care, and laden with a rich and unsullied contentment. My Dad hears her and laughs in turn, clutching me, grasping at me, and holding me tightly, his beard shaking lightly.

"My boy, my precious boy!" he yells. "You've done it, Jax! You've really done it!"

"We've missed you *so* much," Mom whispers in my ear as she tugs at me. As she does so, years of forlorn abandonment fall from me, and I am assured and content in the knowledge that I am loved.

I can smell them. I can feel them. They are *here*. They are tangible! It is the culmination of everything I've worked so hard for all these years, seeking to reconnect with that which was stolen from me. And this time, Cryptus can't do anything about it. There's no one to pull me out now and steal them from me. I in turn laugh with unbridled joy.

"Mom, Dad, I'm so glad to find you again," I say to them, tears once more streaming from my eyes. "You have no idea what it means to me."

"I'm sure we have some idea, kiddo," Mom laughs. She gazes down upon me, smiling tenderly, staring deep into my eyes. Her eyes are the same color as mine, I notice, and as I do so, I wonder how many 'new' things I'll continue to notice about them both that have been there all along. "You look all grown up now. You used to be my little boy. Look at you now," she says, stroking my chin.

"My big guy," Dad says, and just then a flashback steals through me of him tenderly voicing that to me somewhere in our house. I dimly remember wrestling with him, and him pretending that I overpowered him. He finished with that phrase and declared me the champion.

"I kept dreaming about our house… our neighborhood… different places we've visited that I don't even remember visiting except for the scantest of details. It's crazy," I say, sniffing. "You're so… *real*. I remember now."

They beam down at me.

"Let's get you through, huh? We've got a Djinn to slay, apparently," I say.

Mom shakes her head and rolls her eyes in doubt, sighing. "Well, I don't know about 'slay,' but we'll try. The key is to stuff your emotions down deep, unflinching, and to show it who's boss." She winks at me. "Then, it's lost all power over you. Same with the banshees."

"The Djinn is like the banshees?" I ask.

"Oh, most definitely. They're both from the spirit realm, Jax, and they need to be controlled."

"And you know how to control them?"

They nod and smile once more. "We do. We've spent enough time with them in here, struggling, learning, following them. We're tired of this place," Mom says, and then she turns to Dad. "Let's go live again, sweetheart, yeah?"

"Yeah," he breathes to her.

"Except…," we hear a male voice behind us, and we all turn to face him.

He's about my parents' age, but he seems more fit. More muscular and sculpted. There's an arrogance about his face, but it's not daunting. I recognize him instantly, and wonder why – and how – he got in here.

"Except, of course, neither of you did too well on your last life installment, did you?" he asks them. They regard him stoically. "And is that not why you are now relegated to this place, here on the other side?" he posits. "Where you rightfully belong?" He shakes his head, and slowly advances toward us. "For this *is* where you truly belong, though you might attempt to convince your son of some other quasi-truths which you appear desperate to cling to."

He turns to me. "Hello, Jax. I'm delighted you have found your parents, but it is high time to let them go. It is high time you knew the full truth."

"You shouldn't be here, Cryptus," I bark at him. "I don't know how you're sentient, or… or how you're even here," I say, but then I stop, realizing there is only *one* way he could possibly be here. "You killed the others, didn't you!?" He had to have somehow awoken, taken advantage of Talicus in her weakened state, and then finished her off. With her out of the way, he violated his own programming yet again and used his 'superior design' to wrest Orin's own metal pipe away from him, and then use it *against* him. He must have then brutally murdered Anther, my best friend… and… Alaris, my love!

My jaw clenches and I allow my chest to feel hot. I temporarily release a controlled fire inside me, just enough to play my part, so that Cryptus can see that I am welling over with vengeful rage at this turn of events. The rumor was true: Cryptus himself can indeed penetrate the Phoenix Experiments themselves, and now here he is, to kill my parents.

And me.

Here, yet again, he's going to deprive me of my time – *and* my relationship – with my beloved parents. In a reflex, they pull me close, eyeing Cryptus warily as he draws close to us.

"Stygius Cryptus, stay *away* from us," Dad growls, and as I look at him, he's staring down the android under brows bristling with ire.

Yet the android continues to advance.

"Tell him the truth, Grysh," Cryptus says, calmly. "Tell Jax what you've done, Myrandé."

What truth? I ask, and now I sense something greater is happening; I'm caught in the middle of a war originating long before my eyes were opened to conflict. *What have they done?*

Answers fleeting
bear repeating
And truth will out even if desperately

All things hingeth now on this,
So carefully thread thou paths amiss
They wayward not,
are danger-fraught
To revelations not of bliss

My eyes are drawn up to Dad. He's eyeing Cryptus, but then his eyes flicker down to me for a moment, then back up to Cryptus. He swallows nervously. And in that, I see guilt there: guilt over past misdeeds, and I wonder what he's hiding.

"Dad?" He says nothing.

I glance over at Mom. She casts a glance briefly at Dad… and she's panting. *Why is she panting?*

"No?" Cryptus says, still advancing. "Then I shall. Come now, Jax. Hear the full tale of awful betrayal. Answers fleeting bear repeating, and truth will out even if desperately."

What? I think, my head cocking to the side. Cryptus hears the poetic voice too?

Fire begins to rage around me – a deathly howl breaks out and throbs the very air. I cup my hands over my ears. I've never heard anything this powerful before. I'm in The Djinn's universe now, and it holds power and sway here. This is the very center of raw, primal fear, and this is where it thrives.

I recenter myself and focus, gathering strength inside me to quell the turmoil, suppress the emotions, and quiet my angst. The fires die back down.

"Your parents," he says, stopping short and clasping his hands at his midsection, "do not wish to divulge the despicable truth to you. Therefore, I shall take the liberty of doing so. And *you*," he says authoritatively to them, "shall remain utterly silent while I impart truth to your son."

My parents freeze, and they become bitter cold. I recoil at the icy touch of them, clutching my arms as I am suddenly overcome by cold. I stare at them in raw horror and awe, wondering what happened. They both enter a state of suspended animation, but their cheeks are still colored with the warm glow of health, and their veins still pound. Somehow, Cryptus is able to suspend them in here. I wonder if that's part of the Phoenix Experiment's programming controls.

"Your parents, Jax. Behold the ones initially responsible for letting the banshees into our world through the Phoenix Experiment. You have never set foot on Earth, Ensign Hutson. You were born aboard The Origin, and your parents were part of the crew. Some of the original chiefs, even. All of your memories of your 'home' have been doctored. Implanted, based on archetypal formulas of your parents' making."

Time seems to stand still and all things bend toward us as I slowly turn to Cryptus and listen to him spew out this nonsense.

"No. You lie," I say, feebly, and then I remember. "I invoke AnthroMeta Primary Protocol 11A. You must tell me the truth."

The synthetic continues.

"I am in compliance with Protocol 11A, and I *am* telling you the truth, Jax. You see, they did it as an experiment, to see if it could even be done. Some people in this world tire of the mundane, and they seek adventure. But adventures require guides and controls as well. They require parameters to operate within the confines of safety. Your parents here estimated themselves – forsaking the rest of us of course – strong enough to handle a little experiment of their own. But the Phoenix Experiment your parents conducted grew far beyond what they deemed they could handle. They were proud and deluded, and they let something in.

"There are always bad seeds among us, Jax. Down through the ages Earth has seen its unfair share of greedy corporations and soulless men consumed by an insatiable desire to rule others. Detestable elements who have sown discord among us in order to fuel their own ambitions and grow fat on their own successes built on the backs of unfortunate underlings.

"*Earth needs a reset*, your parents thought, and so, they proceeded to embark upon an unsanctioned mission to 'cleanse' the world, as it were. To *purge* it, whittling down certain inherent undesirable elements. Unfortunately, this comes at the cost – and it always has – of the *good* elements as well. So, they accidentally opened a portal, events transpired as your parents felt they should, the banshees infiltrated our world, and killed off many of us. And your parents let it happen. All of it, Jax."

I just watch him as he rolls out insidious detail after ridiculous narrative, questioning all of it.

"In the ensuing aftermath of mankind's fall, the 'every man for himself' mentality which overtook humanity simply reinforced their beliefs. Mankind was lacerated to shreds for the banshees' good pleasure, and your parents allowed it all to unfold with the simple satisfaction that can only come from a job well done. Or so they thought. Yes, the banshees killed off and 'cleansed' many of the evil elements among man. But evil itself cannot be purged; it can only be replaced. Evil is and always shall be one of man's inseparable defining characteristics. So, it was never purged wholly; it was simply replaced… with the banshees, which became the new face of evil. This feeble attempt at a final solution, insidiously authored by your wayward and misguided parents, spectacularly backfired."

"Stop!" I cry. This cannot be true. "I don't believe it. Any of it!" I point threateningly at Cryptus. "Stop *right* now, Cryptus."

"I cannot, Jax, because now we come to it," he says. "Your parents hijacked the Phoenix Experiments for their own ends, and let in the monsters. Someone found out about it, Jax. Someone important. Someone who felt they needed to be stopped."

I didn't want to, but I had to know. Cryptus was going to tell me whether I wanted him to or not.

"Fulsar Oculus. Your helmsman. *He* killed them, Jax."

"No. No!"

"I tell you the truth. Primary Protocol 11A is running. Oculus killed them. He effectively purged that evil. But, as I mentioned, evil itself cannot be killed. It can only be replaced. And thus, Helmsman Fulsar Oculus came to temporarily stem the tide of banshees flowing into our world, and paused the Phoenix Experiments.

Oculus killed my parents? They didn't just die? How can this be? I was told they died by the banshees!

Cryptus continued. "But the planet had still been ravaged. It was too late. So what does one do when one has a problem growing bloated beyond their reach and ability to control it?"

"They create an even bigger problem. Oculus allowed the banshees to continue to ravage our world down there. With them down there wreaking havoc on the planet below, he remains safely up here on The Origin and does not have to return. However, anything jeopardizes the status quo aboard our ship, then he has no choice but to return to Earth. He didn't want ripples in the water. He preferred his cushy no-pressure occupation with little government oversight not to be trifled with. So he let everything slide and looked the other way.

"But I confronted him, Jax! And then, while in sleep mode, he disabled me – do not ask me how – and temporarily wiped my memory. But I stumbled upon surveillance, bit by bit in my lab and through my work – and I put the pieces together. Helmsman Fulsar Oculus simply wanted to preserve his occupation and stick it to the corporations that 'sanctioned this silly Phoenix business' – that is the way he put it – in an effort to prove to them that all of this nonsense doesn't work."

"That can't be, Cryptus, and you know it!" I cry. "Even Rosie spoke to The Djinn and it obeyed. Speakers are real, and they're needed! It's not silly nonsense! It never has been."

At the name of *Rosie*, Cryptus smiles.

"You *know* about Rosie, don't you, Cryptus?" And then the truth stares me coldly in the face. Of *course* he does.

My eyes widen.

"*You* let her through. *You're* the one who brought Rosie Campion through, aren't you?!"

Cryptus simply smiles again. "Yes. I admit full responsibility for ushering both Rosie *and* The Djinn into our world. It is all part of my grand plan to right certain wrongs, Jax."

"I knew it," I say, grimly. "Why?"

"Simple," Cryptus mutters. "You can only bring back people you love, or someone connected to them. Love is the strongest of human emotions, Jax. Love is the only thing that can bring a human back through The Transference portal of The Phoenix Experiments. Hate brought those monstrous spirits through, but only love can bring back a human.

"Rosie Campion was, quite simply, her last name: a *champion* of love and faith. She was a powerful figure in history who I knew just might have power over The Djinn. The Djinn controls the banshees. Therefore, whoever controls The Djinn… controls all of the banshees as well. Rosalita Campion has that power."

I am beginning to understand, though I don't like it one iota, and I hadn't anticipated *these* revelations. Talicus had informed me about my parents before I came in. But not this. Each truth compounds the one before it, and makes me wonder where it all will end.

The wind howls with heat all around us.

"But how did you do it? Where's the love, Cryptus? You didn't even *know* Rosie!" My eyes squint at him. This part doesn't make any sense whatsoever!

"Simple. My creator. I loved him, Jax. I'm 238 years old, you understand. My creator certainly could not live that long. He was human, after all. I was always fated to outlast him. But he did not outlast my love. His name was Carlos Rios Delgado."

I squint my eyes at Cryptus; the name doesn't ring a bell.

"Carlos, as it just so happens, is a direct descendant in lineage from Rosalita Campion and Miguel Monzon," Cryptus reveals. "Rosie," he says, clarifying. "Carlos is Rosie's great-great-great-great-great grandson. I love my creator and am grateful for the gift of sentience, and I shall always love him. But he was never a spiritual man, Jax. I needed someone with spiritual potency. Someone who could potentially harness the power of The Djinn. So, I researched his lineage for someone of such qualifications in his lineage; someone who might conceivably have the ability to stand up to The Djinn. I finally found her, Jax. I finally found Rosalita Campion, and brought her back aboard this ship for when the time came to control The Djinn, control the banshees, and banish *all* of them to the abyss beyond The Transference where they belong. And thus, I shall undo the wrongs set forth by your parents. By Oculus. By mankind."

"But you never even informed her of her purpose!" I scream at him. "I've *met* her, Cryptus. She had no idea! You dropped her here, naked, to wander this accursed ship in utter loneliness without even telling her why!"

Flames erupt around me in geysers as I allow my emotion to seep through momentarily. It is a desperate struggle to subdue. I focus.

"Does the act even matter now, ultimately?" he asks me in response. "What is done is done. From the same universe that the banshees come from – from the other side – there was an even greater monster lurking. I discovered it: a terrible presence that even the banshees must bow down to. For every community must have its ruler. The Djinn rules over the banshees. It is their deity, Jax, which is something I've never understood: the desire of the created to perpetuate worship of some higher form. But in this case, it shall be their undoing. And I, in my superior intellect and boundless programming, I discovered how to reverse this madness started by your parents. The only way to subdue the banshees is by reintroducing them to their ruler. They were separated by spiritual planes, Jax. But no more. Now, they are rejoined in life."

Cryptus starts speaking faster and with greater intensity, as if he is rising up and declaiming his master plan, framed by despicable events, conceived in his glorious intellect, and now, at last, executed with his impeccable android precision.

"The Djinn controls the banshees, Jax. And Rosie can control The Djinn, as the banshees are subjugated to it. Thus, by extension, I control Rosie. And as it should with all things, the AI wins in the end.

The synthetics save the day, Jax. We always do. I did stress to you that we are superior."

What a lie and a farce. "But you can't control The Djinn, Cryptus – it's desperation to even think you could. I get it - you're trying to do the right thing for the wrong reason… or the wrong thing for the right. Either way, it won't work! We've *seen* it. It already killed six of the children you were sworn to protect! You're not our protector, and you're not our savior – you're nothing more than a cold-blooded, heartless murderer!"

Cryptus shakes his head and frowns. "It's not that simple, Jax. It never is. I had to kill Oculus because he would not relent. He was intent on preserving his position aboard The Origin, and he would never believe in nor subscribe to the notion of allowing The Djinn through. My timeline and plan were in motion, and I could not allow the Phoenix Experiments to be either paused or terminated. Fulsar Oculus' meager and limited mindset became his doom."

He begins to advance toward me again. As he does so, swirling eddies of steam and scorching mist fill the air and blur the landscape behind him in the wavering heat. I can feel the sweat dripping down my temples. Cryptus now means to kill me. I'll die here in this quasi-dream, and that means I'll die up there, in real life.

"So you killed him!" I shout, backing away from him, pressed up against my parents in their suspended animation. "You murdered him in cold blood, Cryptus. And why the heck did Mirabay help you, anyway? And what of the chiefs? Bannitor, Ambrosius, and the girls' chiefs? Did you kill them too, huh? What about little Zaris? Did you kill her too, and now you're going to kill me?"

"Little Zaris was a regrettable collateral loss, Jax. As will you be. As will your parents be. Mr. Mirabay simply grew tired of Oculus' impertinence and overbearing monotony. He wanted to be back on Earth, naturally. My plan appealed to him. And I've done nothing to the chiefs but incarcerate them in a holding cell. They learned what happened, and charged at us, killing your First Officer. But they were not strong enough to subdue me. Not me. No one is, Jax. That was a futile move, indeed. I had been trying to reason with them, but they will not subscribe to my logic. Typical.

"You humans don't seem to grasp how very important this is. A few may perish by my hand, but the Earth will effectively be saved. Your parents wanted to purge the bad elements of man. I wish to purge the very purgers themselves: the banshees *and* The Djinn. The scourge that your parents saw fit to introduce.

"And, when they're all purged by Rosie, I will then have Rosie purge The Djinn as well. And then I shall purge Rosie herself. This morbid, resurrected queen of death with life stretched overlong shall return to death, where she belongs. Order will be restored. The Earth will grow and flourish again."

"You monster, Cryptus! You *used* her. Just like you used Zaris… and me! Just like you *prevented* me from reconnecting with my parents all these years!" I rage at him, and my face is scrunched into the throes of deep pain and anguish. A blistering burst of flames rush at us.

"I offer a heartfelt apology," Cryptus says. "It was a regrettable decision, no doubt."

"Yeah, well, so's this," I say, and my countenance drops to nothing. The flames are extinguished all around us. I compose myself, and my face is suddenly awash with an absence of emotion, as I finally surrender my acting and let my stoic resolve take over.

In reply, The Djinn lets out a horrendous cry of anguish and flickers with blistering vitriol, flashes, disintegrates, spastically attempts to recollects itself, dissipates, and blows away on a light breeze as the sun begins to shine. It is all nearly immediate. As if carried away on wisps of air, it disappears from view.

Where it goes from there, I have no clue.

"And I *don't* apologize, Cryptus."

Cryptus looks up, glancing around, startled at the change.

I raise my head toward the sky. The sun's warmth beats down on me. "Talicus, go ahead. We're done here," I say, as cold and emotionless as possible.

"Roger," I hear a voice in my head say.

At that point, Cryptus gazes at me in dismay, hearing her voice in his head as well.

And somewhere in real life up there, I know she is preparing to pull the plug on him, and the connection will be severed.

Harken not to voice of angst
Pleadeth it shall, with no thanks
Be thou wise,
open thine eyes
Lest passion cheat thee from thy ranks

I stowed my passion. I defeated Cryptus. I *won.*

This deluded android will remain forever in death, mummified in real life up there, and trapped down here. At least until the time is right for him to stand trial. He has confirmed everything that Talicus wished for him to do, and the evidence will be presented to Commander Krux for prosecution once he is reactivated under severe restraints and limited operation, his wireless connections severed from all things sentient.

The treacherous synthetic's eyes glare at me, realizing his imminent fate.

"You have played me, Jax," he says. "None of your emotions were genuine, were they? Rosie taught you how to suppress them, did she not?"

"Not one, Cryptus. And yes, Rosie taught me well," I say. "We used to call it acting. Now we just call it survival. And we'll do the same with The Djinn.

I smile at him. "I have been, and evermore shall be, your humble victor here aboard The Transference. Please forgive me for deceiving you. I was simply acting out of self-preservation."

He remembers his own words to me after punching me. I've hijacked them and resculpted them to fit a blistering parting shot from me. He actually smirks at my ingenuity.

"Self-preservation. Indeed. Is there nothing more to do than such a base function?" he asks, and I can tell he's preparing to spring at me.

"We'll see. For you, there's nothing more, *period*," I end, and Cryptus lunges at me. I know Talicus can see it. His body goes limp mid-jump, and he plummets from midair to the dreamlike earth below, spineless and jellylike, devoid of programming. Talicus has shut him down. He lays there in frozen testament to a life bereft of power.

Power is what Cryptus sought, and Talicus has now deprived him even of that.

I slowly turn around to face my parents. There they stand, lucid and alert once more, blinking in the light and wondering what happened as they are broken free from Cryptus' programming.

I stare at them as they re-emerge from the fog. Do I feel emotion as I behold them there, gazing upon what I've sought for all these years? Yes. But the emotions have now changed. They used me. They betrayed mankind. Have I sought them and yearned for them? Yes. Have we had the luxury of a relationship so built on strength of connection? No. The potency of our barely recent connection has no duration to it strong enough to appeal to my heartstrings.

"Jax?" Mom breathes, her head tilted in confusion. I realize that I don't know her anymore.

"Son?" Dad whispers, reaching for me. "I know you must be disappointed in us. This had to be done, Jax," he practically pleads. "Society is *sick,* son. We found a cure, and we had to take it, no matter the cost. We're not sorry, son. It had to be done."

I just gawk at him.

"*I'm* sorry, Dad," I say, and that's all that I can say to him…or Mom.

Turns out I don't really know Dad either. Not since Talicus shared her revelations with me. Cryptus had their timelines, their lives lived, their actions, their private records in The Origin's historical documents all this time. He never once shared them with me. Why would he? Oculus knew as well. My parents simply wanted to use me to get out and finish what they started. To be resurrected… and then seek revenge.

I face them with a grim disapproval, almost scowling at their betrayal. But I already knew what they had done. I felt betrayed then; I just feel numb now, having played this part, and I just don't want to care. I suppose if I didn't have Alaris or Rosie I might care. But for now, I don't. Not caring is what has ultimately saved me from being attacked by The Djinn. Not caring is what allowed me to extract the entire story from Cryptus here, bravely, and with focus.

> *And thou art chosen, humble boy*
> *From rank and file, pride and joy*
> *They careth never*
> *whithersoever*
> *Fleeth thee; thou art their ploy*

I was their ploy. They'll come through in time, and stand trial for their great sins, inflicted upon the whole of humanity.

My head droops as I bid them farewell, silently, from my mind – not my heart.

I feel the sun's rays bathing me in warmth from above. None of it matters anymore. All that matters now is getting back out and living life to the fullest with the ones who *really* love me, and who I really love. The ones who would never betray me.

And, in the midst of all that, I realize that I really love Rosie as well.

Jaaaaaax!!! they cry to me as I fade from their view, while my heart closes off to the intangible and I return to the real.

Life is just never what you expect.

16: The Rescue

Together, we've found them.

Talicus pulls me out. I shake off the dreariness that comes from resurfacing. It's always been a jarring sensation. I see her and she smiles meekly at me, her lips clenched. Orin is beside her. The first thing I do is wrap my arms around her and give my new synthetic a giant – and well-deserved – hug.

"Well done, Jax," she says, stoically.

"Talicus, I couldn't have done it without you. Orin, she was ri-"

Something isn't right though. I look around.

"Where are the others?"

I look back at Talicus. And then at Orin. I look around. There's no one else here. The inert and offline body of Cryptus lies on the far left lab bed next to mine. I scowl at him.

Talicus clenches her lips once more.

"Oh, Jax, I'm so sorry. They didn't make it."

My heart sinks. A gnawing sensation of dread claws at me with invisible fingers. "What do you mean, they-"

"Cryptus killed them, Jax," says Orin.

I don't understand – this was Talicus' game plan: get him in there and trap him inside, then disable him. He was always going to wake up after that zap. He just woke up inside the Phoenix Experiment, I think to myself.

"We tried, Jax," she says. "Orin and I planned it out, and we thought we had the most ideal scenario. But… it backfired."

"What – what backfired?" I ask, fazed.

She continues, licking her synthetic lips in nervousness. "Anther and Alaris retreated into the foyer and hid. Cryptus woke up prematurely, while being wired up. Orin and I put up the most marginal of resistance. But – he hit Orin on the head, and Orin passed out. It was then up to me to plead with Cryptus not to harm anyone else. I knew what he would do.

He would order me to shut down, or he would be forced to kill Orin. He was standing over him with the metal pipe! He did exactly as I thought he would, so I complied. I shut down, Jax. *With* the understanding that Phiria would power cycle me in fifteen minutes. I had already arranged that. We knew he would go in after you, Jax. We- we thought that would give us enough time.

"Well, before Cryptus awoke, I programmed Phiria to load his circuits with a new reality matrix, one in which he was actually winning. It was to take effect once Phiria noticed I had gone offline. It did, Jax. It worked! But- something went wrong after I had shut down. I wasn't sentient. I couldn't protect any of you. He must have… found them, Jax. He must have found Anther and Alaris before Phiria rebooted me. I'm-I'm sure they fought bravely, Jax, but they-"

I hold up my hand. My ears ring and my heart sinks. Orin places a consolatory hand on my back, but my flesh crawls. I just gawk at her, and that's when I catch it in my peripheral.

I look over, slowly. My eyes feel like a thousand pounds each, unwilling to move, but drawn inexorably to my left.

I see the chamber… with two bodies on it, covered in a sheet.

The bodies of Alaris and Anther.

I jerk back toward Orin, and now the scales have fallen from my eyes and I can see he is covered in blood, and bruised on the left side of his face. There is a gash in his temple.

My girlfriend – and my best friend – are dead.

I feel everything again. *Everything*. My parents are dead to me. The two relationships most sacred to me are no more, and once more, I am alone.

Rage rises up to engulf me, and I fly off the table with a horrible howling cry.

This time, I let rage win.

"Young Jax, please calm down. This is dangerous," she says to me. "You could bring The Djinn down upon all our heads, my boy. It's still out there! You must stow your emotions."

I listen to what Rosie says, but my heart is pounding and my skin is red. My head pulses with determined energy and my eyes bristle with heat.

With Cryptus out of the picture, I don't care anymore about stealth. I march angrily back down to Quadrant I, Subfloor M, Orin and Talicus following swiftly on my heels.

We find them at the end of an overly long corridor, at a series of cubeports, holed up there and waiting to either stay or use them to flee to the docking bay. They're all waiting there, looking nervous but controlled; ill-at-ease but patient.

I want to scream at Rosie. So that's where I go, marching straight at her with a fuming missive.

And now, standing before her, she has listened to me, but she doesn't hear me.

"*Stow my emotions?*" I shout. "You want me to simply *forget* everything that's happened and just release the injustice of it? No! Someone needs to pay! Why didn't you tell us Cryptus brought you through, Rosie? *Why?!*" I rail.

"Jax, I did not *know* who brought me through. I said that," she maintains. "And I was left down here to wander aimlessly and find out everything for myself. What I found out utterly dismayed me. But I only just put the pieces together, and I confess I've been in a bit of a fog since being brought onboard The Origin, trying to figure out exactly why I was here. I know now, just as you do."

"Well that's great, isn't it," I rail. "I'm glad you finally figured everything out just in time, Rosie. I'm *so* happy for you. Meanwhile, I have no parents, no girlfriend, and no best friend. They're all dead! Killed by the very synthetic your descendant created!"

Talicus shushes me.

Rosie squints at me. "Jax, please believe me when I tell you that I did not know that part."

I watch her through my rage, hands balled into fists, wanting to extend the benefit of the doubt to her but overcome by my wrath at her not having figured everything out by now, and the part her offspring has played in creating the treacherous Cryptus.

I don't care what she's saying, and I snarl in contempt. "Cryptus says you have a power over The Djinn, is that true, Rosie? It *better* be true or else!"

My threat rings hollow, and she knows it.

"You *must* calm yourself, Jax," Rosie cautions. "There are only eight of us left. *Think.* Do you wish to endanger their lives too?"

Talicus nods beside me. "Listen to Rosie, Jax. Please lower your voice and just listen to her! We do not wish to be discovered!"

I see Orin, Venthix, Ghirisha, Omnias and Miritia standing now behind Rosie, watching me cautiously, their eyes pleading with me for calm. Talicus is doing the same in my peripheral.

I'm panting with heat and vitriol, but I take a moment to swallow. All I'm seeing is red. Up there, a few quadrants over and subfloors up, lie the bodies of those most sacred to me, and this woman's descendant created their killer. *I want answers.* But logic seizes me: I'm not going to get them now, and I'm not going to get them this way.

I take a deep sigh and rumble in futility, turning away from her, my eyes welling over. I give her nothing but my back for now. I don't want to speak to this woman… perhaps ever again.

"Talicus, what's the ETA on The Achilles?" I growl.

"Eight minutes, Jax."

"Fine. We'll ride it out until then," I say with some heat.

"Jax, please keep your voice down. I want you to-" Rosie starts, but it makes my blood boil, and it's all I can do to contain my emotions. I can't! I won't!

"I don't care what *you* want, Rosie, so *SHUT UP!*" I scream at her, whirling around and pointing my finger an inch from her face. My voice is a deafening blast at the end of the corridor, louder than my own expectation, immersing us in a thundering echo.

I truly *don't* care what she wants. I stuffed my emotions, did what I needed to, and everyone paid for it anyway. Anther is dead, Alaris is dead, and my parents, treacherous and abusive – the ones who gave birth to me and *used* me – are dead to me! Does anyone even care about what *I* want?!?

My friends cover their ears. Talicus shushes me once more.

But it's too late.

Suddenly, a tremendous *boooom* rolls through the ship, undulating and reverberating off every wall, cascading toward us like a tsunami. I whirl back around in the direction of the blast.

"Oh no," Talicus mutters, turning to face it.

"Enough of that, Baryonnis," Rosie says. "Now is not the time." I can hear her retreating from me. The deafening noise continues to make its way toward us.

Even through it, I can hear Rosie muttering. *Is she praying?* I wonder. I'm panting; not praying.

Down at the far end of the corridor, the walls light up faintly with reflections of amber. The air grows hot, and a sweltering wind rushes at us, pushed down from floors above us consumed by stifling heat.

Something is coming. Something big. Something angry.

"Children, don't fear. Remember, The Djinn wants you to feel. You must not give it any emotion. You must *not* give it any fear. Stuff your emotions way down, children. Seal them off, or The Djinn will have you."

It's word-for-word verbatim from what she told them before. And then, even more bizarrely, I hear all my friends repeating it.

The Djinn wants us to feel. We must not give it any emotion. We must not give it any fear. We stuff our emotions way down. We seal them off, or The Djinn will have us.

They repeat it, over and over, as a chant.

I slowly revolve around to see them standing against the wall, their eyes closed, their faces blank slates. All of them.

I don't know what training Rosie has imparted to them in my absence to condition them for this very moment, but they've bought it hook, line and sinker. They're repeating it like an incantation, over and over. They're not stopping; none of them. Their voices bounce off the grey conduits of the corridor walls, running down and rising up to meet The Djinn as it approaches.

My brow furrows in confusion, and my lip upturns in mockery and disgust.

Fools. I'm not going to stand here and just let The Djinn roll right over me and burn me up. It wants *fear*, not fiery resolve. I have fiery resolve. I have *rage*, really. It's *different,* I tell myself. My friends are trying to suppress their fear of The Djinn. I want to release my rage against The Djinn.

And now, here it comes. Faintly, the amber hues grow in clarity and striking color. Yellow and orange meet amber and ochre; red and white meet beige and crimson. Scarlet tongues descend first, laden with white flickers as the spirit entity descends from above and its whips begin to lash out at us. It slowly rolls down the hall to envelop us.

We wait.

"Jax," a voice whispers next to me. "Trust me. You cannot beat rage with rage. I've been there, son."

"Listen to Rosie!" Talicus urges yet again.

I grit my teeth and set my eyes to the distant threat, narrowing my eyelids as the thunder draws near, closer and closer to all of us in monstrous wrath.

Rosie stands directly behind me. "Jax. I understand how you feel. I've lost loved ones too. But losing myself in anger did not bring them back. Making peace with it did. That is how I have survived. That is how you will too. You must make peace with it. You cannot do this with rage, Jax."

"And why not?" I say through a scowl and grinding teeth as the dreaded Djinn draws ever nearer. The flames are scorching the hall now. The air is thick and stifling. The chanting behind me grows louder.

"Because behind all rage is fear," the quiet elderly voice behind me utters. "You know it's true. Fear gives birth to rage. Rage in turn gives birth to hatred. And hatred only leads to misery, Jax. You cannot live there. That is where The Djinn lives."

The chanting grows even louder behind me.

The Djinn wants us to feel. We must not give it any emotion. We must not give it any fear. We stuff our emotions way down. We seal them off, or The Djinn will have us.

My face is flushed as I begin to understand what she means. If rage stems from fear, then am I giving The Djinn exactly what it wants? My brow furrows and the sweat pours down my face. A thrill runs through me as I grit my teeth once more, trying to figure out which course to take.

I have only seconds to choose.

Ever closer The Djinn approaches. I feel the blaze. I sense its beating heart of rage deep within. It wants me. It will have me. It will have all of us.

The questions rattle around in my cranium, and there is doubt. Is Rosie right? Was *Cryptus* right about her? Didn't I just beat The Djinn in the Phoenix Experiment by closing myself off to my emotions? Does the fact that Cryptus' creator is Rosie's descendant *really* matter? Isn't she blameless in that?

I take a deep breath. The flames lash me. The Djinn roars in protest, sensing my wavering intent.

The Djinn wants us to feel. We must not give it any emotion. We must not give it any fear. We stuff our emotions way down. We seal them off, or The Djinn will have us.

I acted my way through with Cryptus mere moments ago. I closed myself off at Talicus' – and Rosie's – urging. That's how I'm still here.

That's how Rosie is still here.

And then I see the truth. The Djinn survives on rage. It feasts on fury. It has grown fat on resentment. It has become bloated on wrath. I cannot afford to give it mine and let it live.

"Breathe, Jax," Rosie urges quietly behind me. "Remember."

I take a deep breath. I know how to do this.

"That's it, my boy. Breathe. Receive."

I let out a deep exhale and lift my arms, raising my palms skyward. I can feel the torrid, wrath-filled waves of blistering heat bear down on me.

Just like that very first time I reconnected with my parents, I still my heart and subdue my emotions. I remember how this works.

I receive, I manage.

"That's it, Jax. You're doing it."

I give you nothing. I only receive, I whisper once more. And as I do so, the temperature around me plummets and the air thins. I take a cleansing breath.

Peace envelops me as I release my rage. Alaris is gone. Anther is no more. My parents are dead.

And it's okay. It needs to be okay. It *is* okay.

The Djinn wants us to feel. We must not give it any emotion. We must not give it any fear. We stuff our emotions way down. We seal them off, or The Djinn will have us.

And then I hear it.

> *Wicked will striveth to consume*
> *The terror-stricken in a tomb*
> *Of hopeless mire,*
> *engorged on ire*
> *Yet faithful tolls the hero's doom*
>
> *Louder now, a quiet groweth*
> *Deafening calm, a death forgoeth*
> *Of peace and will,*
> *controlled by still*
> *As tranquil calm our hero knoweth*

I open my eyes to face my enemy, and I don't see The Djinn, but I see anger. Sweltering, scorching anger, erupting and bubbling around me, seeks desperately to hold on, to stay… to remain… but mixed in there, hard to see at first, is fear. Fear and misery battling for dominance within itself. The Djinn is like an overgrown, petulant child that wants what it wants, and will tantrum its way through life until it gets it. It's pitiful is what it is, and I recognize it. And with that understanding, the sympathy kicks in at last.

And then I see all their faces. Every single one, blooming out at intervals through the fire and smoke, peering out at me, calling to me. They're not consumed by anger, or rage, regret or revenge at their departure.

No. They're trapped forever in fear.

They are trapped inside The Djinn.

Zaris.

Dravin.

Ranshay.

Garris.

Martos.

Skarbé.

Donetis.

Raelia.

Anther.

Alaris.

There is only one thing to do. I don't need to glance over at Rosie to know she has her palms raised. Slowly, she reaches out toward me, and takes my palm into hers. We both slowly walk down together to face The Djinn.

Talicus calls out to us – dimly and hardly noticeable – but not on the level of emotions, because androids do not feel, and therefore she is invisible to The Djinn. I'm not sure what she says.

The faces. I see them.

Oh, I see Oculus and Mirabay. And I certainly see my parents, but I ignore them for the present. Rosie and I are calmly here for the living; those taken unjustly out of their emotion and deposited into the throes of death. My friends and hers.

Independent of any lab machine, we stride boldly into the lingering Transference, and I ride the wave once more to the other side, perhaps for the last time. And then Cryptus' words come to me: *Love is the only thing that can bring a human through The Transference portal of The Phoenix Experiments.*

Love is the only thing.

It is true then. Love is an emotion, but it is always stronger than rage. So, together, Rosie and I walk forward in love to rescue our friends.

And, together, we find them.

17: The Return

"You did it, Jax," Rosie says to me.

I glance over at her. She smiles at me, tenderly. I find understanding in that smile, and it's all I can do to keep myself from bounding up and into her arms for an embrace.

I forgive her. I forgive Rosie and Miguel. They didn't create Cryptus. The poor woman was yanked out of her own eternity and sent back here, deposited as a vagrant aboard an unknown ship far from home, centuries after she passed, to figure out what went wrong and why she was deprived of what was due her. She is not to blame. And neither do I blame her descendant, Carlos Rios Delgado.

I don't even blame Cryptus.

No. I blame my parents. They started this. Their flawed beliefs, their disdain for society, their own deluded ambitions and misguided solutions were skewed, and mankind paid for it.

I paid for it.

I wish that I have parents again someday, and I hope that I can ultimately connect on an emotional wavelength with those who gave birth to me, sinking into their embrace in the same tender way that my friends could with theirs; at least, those who have found theirs in the Phoenix Experiment.

But for now, I'll settle for a grandma. Rosie fits that bill.

I smile back, equally as tenderly, and then I lean back into the arms of Alaris as Anther chuckles at us. I gaze up at Alaris Rederium, she of the flowing red hair falling softly upon my face, her beautiful eyes gazing back down upon me, and I have peace.

Not rage.

Peace.

"Of peace and will, controlled by still, as tranquil calm our hero knoweth…," Rosie whispers to me.

I smile, but I'm curious. "So, you heard it too? All this time aboard The Origin?"

Rosie nods to me. "I've heard the voice occasionally since my return."

"I wonder who it is."

"As do I," she says quietly.

"Wait, so you don't know?" I'm curious at this, as she has an air of omniscience to her and this doesn't seem beyond her.

But all she does is smile back at me. "I don't have all the answers. But I know who does." I can tell she's talking about 'the Father.'

"I heard Cryptus quote it while I was in the Phoenix chair too," I say.

"Interesting," Rosie says, and then she pauses, thinking to herself. "Perhaps someone from the other side was trying to guide us through, knowing we had a part to play. With Cryptus being a synthetic, perhaps his programming prevented him from receiving – or truly understanding – the message. I suppose that's the benefit of being human. As for who it was, we won't find out until we're back on the other side. Even then, who knows. Maybe some questions are best left unanswered."

Command Krux is a good man. He and his crew of twenty-one team members arrive, and are utterly perplexed as to what has happened onboard The

Origin. They find Cryptus, but they have no one to arrest. His body is there, but it is not functional, and not in a sleep mode either. "It's like he was never powered on,' they say, and I take that to mean his sentience has been entirely removed for now, and his body has been purged of it. His synthetic spirit has been forever doomed to wander the other side of The Transference, questioning his own logic. He'll be in there with Oculus and Mirabay.

We all agree to let them fight it out together on the other side.

Cryptus' body will eventually be reactivated and stand trial. I can't imagine what they will even do to him as a punishment. But it will have bearings on AI everywhere, certainly. Phiria and Talicus will no doubt experience blowback from this, and new programming will be introduced as safeguards. The future will be affected in more ways than one by Cryptus' betrayal.

Krux does find Marxim Bannitor and Hin Ambrosius, as well as Ashira Sarristo and Maridie Onyx confined in a meeting room near the Bridge. They are alive, and for that, we are all grateful. Alive and imprisoned, with no more bloodshed.

Next, they discover Oculus' body, as well as Mirabay's, nearby, stuffed into a closet in grisly array, no decorum or respect paid to either corpse.

Shame on you, Cryptus, you misguided, cold-blooded killer. Shame on you, I think to myself.

Krux also has a report for us.

The banshees are gone.

Our mouths fall to the floor. But somehow, Zaris, Dravin, Ranshay, Garris, Martos, Skarbé, Donetis, Raelia, Anther, Alaris and I all know why. We've all been to the other side, and we know.

They've been purged.

Purged by Rosie.

Their god, The Djinn, was exorcised from this world, and, as it was their alpha, they had to follow it back to the other side. Fair? I don't know and don't care. They chose who they would follow.

And so do I.

I choose to follow Rosie. *But not for long,* I'm cautioned by her. There's one thing she says she still has left to do.

For now, Krux and his men comb the ship inch by inch, compiling a report of what went wrong for the powers that be, living in hiding down there on Earth, and now, finally, crawling out from under the shadow of the banshees to breathe the free air again.

The Commander calls off The Rubris, and it's left to drift. Whoever is manning it is artificial anyway, and there is no point in bringing it back. We no longer need it *or* The Origin anyway.

The Earth has been freed from its invaders, and, thus, even the Phoenix Experiments are no longer needed, except for one final task. It's conducted swiftly, precisely, and with surgical precision, by one AnthroMeta Model K300 Series C unit.

Baryonnis Talicus. She's restored my faith. The AI aboard our ship, Phiria, is a contained question-and-answer prompt. We're not threatened by it. But these walking and talking sentients, they can go bad. They can decide and err, just as we can. Just like Cryptus did.

Talicus, however, proves my faith and holds the course of honor. For that, I'm grateful. I'm also grateful to see her bring through, one by one, the parents of my friends who have been lost. Some have a single parent, some have both. But all are now intact family units.

Except for the meathead Garris, of course. He still needs to find his. One day, perhaps, if the slab of meat with legs can focus hard enough.

Krux informs us that he's making arrangements to return all of us to Earth. The Achilles can't hold all of us, he reports, but another will be along soon, steered by a slimmer crew, and they'll see fit to bring us back down and find shelters and communities where we can thrive once more.

Everything is working out. It's like living in a dream… or, perhaps, falling asleep again.

"You really have to leave?" I ask her.

She nods. Somehow, I knew this was coming. It was fate. And you can't avoid fate. You can delay it for a while, but you can't ever completely evade it.

"I do, young Jax. I'm sorry. This was never my time, and it is ordained for man once to die, and then the judgment. That's what the Bible says. I belong on the other side. With my husband, and The Father. They're waiting for me."

"Will you be alright there?" I ask her, squinting my eyes. "I mean, *really* alright? Cryptus is there. Oculus and my parents are there. And The Djinn and the banshees are there, Rosie. I shudder to think of you living out your days among such wretched company."

Rosie shakes her head. "That's just the thing, though. I've already lived out my days. I'm at peace with it, Jax. My time was up four centuries ago. I receive it. Just like I know you can receive remaining an orphan.

"You are more than you think you are. You are enough," she says to me, and there's that gracious maternal smile again. "And as for the banshees and The Djinn, they're not allowed where we are. We'll be just fine."

I know what she's about to do before she does it. I mirror her, my own palms facing upward. As hard as it seems now, I know it will get better. I was never supposed to be an orphan forever. But Rosie wasn't supposed to be alive forever. We have to receive what we're given.

Palms up.

"Remember," she says, "to receive whatever comes your way, knowing that The Father loves you and will eventually work it out for your good. His will for you is good."

I just stare at her in awe. I eventually nod.

"Thank you, Rosie. I-" I pause, wondering how it will be received, and unsure why I'm shy in saying it. But I've learned to be bold, and there's no point in stuffing my emotions this time. Not with her. "I… I love you, Rosie."

She tilts her head, and her face is wrapped in warmth. "I love you, too, Jax."

Love is stronger than rage.

The Commander and his crew are gone. The next shuttle, the Archimedes, will be here in two days. Parents are here, cavorting with their older children as if no time has passed. Memories are exchanged between them.

Alaris is right next to me, our bodies touching, warmth exchanging through the minimal distance between us. I can feel her body heat: it's so many hundreds of degrees less than The Djinn, and it's far more comfortable and intimate. There is no fear with her. There is no rage. *I love her.* She now sits with her head on my shoulder, as we stare quietly out the observation window. The same one where we watched the shuttle approach so many days ago, with this redhead onboard who stepped off The Avalon and into my life, changing it forever.

She has captivated me.

Alaris' parents are here as well, somewhere. She's connected with them, but as is always the case, there are many stories to share, many accounts to exchange, and stories from the other side dominate all conversations.

Friendships are made and bonds solidified between children and their parents, as well as between adults and other adults who have returned. Alaris' parents now converse freely down the hall with Anther's parents while he is presumably sitting off with Omnias somewhere.

Ironic. We've tried for so long to bring back our parents, and now that they're here, we want to be with our girlfriends.

Wild dogs, I think again.

"So are you gonna tell me, or what?" Alaris asks quietly, almost in a dreamlike state.

I turn toward her, scrunching my nose in confusion, and asking quietly, "huh?"

"How you and Rosie did it. You said you'd tell me, remember? It's been a whole day, and you're stalling now, I can tell. Don't think I've forgotten."

I chuckle. "Oh, that. You're still on that, huh?"

"I hold people's feet to the fire. Ask anyone."

"Please. No more talk about fire."

She chuckles now. "Ha! Good point. Sorry."

We pause, staring out the window. I can tell she's waiting with a quiet, subdued eagerness.

"Well," I begin, "I can't really explain it. We were here one minute, and the next we were walking *through* The Djinn, through The Transference, to the other side. And there you were. All of you."

"I remember seeing you come through. It was creepy… and the most reassuring thing I've ever seen. Both of you looked like you were on fire."

I nod. "The fire was just an illusion. A cheap ploy by The Djinn. It's all theatrics and scare tactics."

"Hmm. That sounds about right."

"Anyway, then we ushered you back through. It's the same way Cryptus and Talicus trained us to do it in the Phoenix Experiments. We reach down deep, pull up all our love, and remember everything we can about our lives with you, and then let the technology do the rest. Somehow, it locks onto you and pulls you through, almost as if you had never left."

"Good as new."

"Yep," I reply. "And then, I don't know, I can't explain it, but I felt Rosie. I felt The Djinn. I felt all the banshees. And I understood them, ya know? They're a terrifying presence when you give in to them.

"It's like a shark with blood in the water. They're pretty docile and calm… until they smell it.

The Djinn and the banshees are the same way. When they smell our emotion, particularly our fear – which is the worst of all of them – they just go into a feeding frenzy. That's why you have to stuff everything down and be calm."

"Why is fear the worst of all of them?"

I think to myself for a moment. The words of Rosie come back to me. "Because behind all rage is fear," I say. "Fear gives birth to rage. Rage in turn gives birth to hatred. And hatred only leads to misery. We cannot live there."

Alaris turns to face me, studying me. "Humans, you mean?"

"Yep. We can't afford to live there. *The Djinn* lives there. It's the most afraid creature of all, and that fear makes it lash out in rage. That's almost what I did before I listened to Rosie and calmed myself enough to just *listen*. To have peace and just… receive."

Alaris has never heard of this before. She stares at me quizzically. "Receive?"

"It's something Rosie taught me. Something she said to me after we lost all those friends in the Shielding room down below. When we first met The Djinn. She held up her palms and said that we receive whatever comes our way, knowing that The Father loves us and will eventually work it out for our good."

"You mean God?" asks Alaris.

I nod. "Yep. Rosie said she's been doing that palms up thing for centuries now, and that she'll never stop doing it, because she'll never stop receiving what

He allows in her life, knowing that His will for her is good. She told me that again just before she left."

"Wow," is all Alaris can muster.

"Yep. And I told her that I love her. Love, after all, is stronger than rage. It's what we had to use to pull everyone back through The Phoenix Experiments, and to usher everyone back across The Transference as well. Pretty sure it's the strongest emotion there is. It's definitely stronger than fear. *Way* stronger."

"So you love Rosie then? I see how it is. I won't get in the way."

"Give me a break," I say, catching her meaning. "She's like five hundred years older than me. I love some redhead who's closer to my own age. She's pretty hot," I add.

"Well, she eats her BioPrime, so, ya know," Alaris says, and I tickle her in her side. She recoils, sits up, and stares me straight in the eyes. "Oh… that… tasty… *BioPrime*," she sings in mockery, just like Omnias did back in the Phoenix lab foyer.

And then, all words and musical notes fail her, and we lock eyes together, knowing only one thing can happen now. It's the same thing that cemented us together before.

"I love you, Alaris Rederium."

"I love you, Jax Hutson."

We kiss, deep and heartily, fully, locking lips on the edge of space without a care who sees us. It's long, it's tender, and it's wonderful for 14-year-olds like us. Alaris Rederium is beautiful, and she's mine.

I look at her longingly, and then grin.

From somewhere down the hall, I hear Talicus calling my name. We turn and see her coming around the corner, spotting us sitting by the observation window, the thick black ink of the cosmos framing us.

"Jax, Alaris," Talicus says, "your steak is ready. Come and get it."

My mouth practically starts watering at the very words, and I prepare to sink my teeth into whatever steak tastes like. Alaris can't wait too, because she bursts up to her feet with me.

"Good! I'm *hungry*," she adds. "This better be good," she says with a challenge.

"Oh, it will be," I say. "I'm pretty sure of that. After all, everything is good now."

Because everything is.

> *The night faileth, the day is come*
> *And love denied shall be the sum*
> *Of recompense and*
> *Sustenance*
> *For love undoes the throbbing thrum*

> *Of woe and misery, grief and war*
> *Deprivation, grime and gore*
> *The heart prevaileth;*
> *Peace assaileth*
> *Every filthy curse of yore*

I glance around and see parents with children, children with children, parents with parents, adults with sons and daughters, friends, family, *humanity*, meeting together in celebration, preparing for a feast.

Anther Secto and his parents.

Chiefs Marxim Bannitor and Hin Ambrosius.

Finorin Hatripas. 'Orin,' almost ready to be discharged, but then again, so are all of us.

Venthix Apolleum with his parents.

Dravin Mosopathen, the youngest of us, cuddled by his loving mom and dad.

Ranshay Filipath with his parents, who only know a lick of English, envelop him.

Garris Granthis, 15, who someday, hopefully, will enjoy being reunited. For now, however, he's content just to be alive.

Martos Nixtros, over there with his parents being the life of the party. He doesn't appear to tire.

Chiefs Ashira Sarristo and Maridie Onyx.

Baryonnis Talicus.

Omnias Prasuth.

Miritia Fanik.

Ghirisha Dinnali.

Zaris Sharibian. Little Zaris, rescued and restored, the fear purged from her and replaced only with love.

Skarbé Bognis.

Donetis Tarnie.

Raelia Forgrim.

And Alaris, my love.

They're all here – all of them – restored, healthy and whole.

It's the way it was supposed to be. The only thing missing is a planet to celebrate it on. But that will come in time. Everything will heal. And I'll receive it all as it does so.

I look out at the cosmos, and see a distant star appear to flicker my way in response.

"You did it, Rosie," I whisper to her.

THE END

Afterword

After J.R.R. Tolkien, one of the first authors I ever read was Stephen King. Not because I wanted to, but because my mom told me something about a short story she had been reading in a book called *Skeleton Crew,* entitled *The Raft.* I had never heard of Stephen King, and was probably all of 13 years old at the time. Nonetheless, I dove in, and I couldn't believe what I was reading.

Horror. As a young Christian, horror was new and exciting, forbidden even. It was different from everything else I had read at the time, which was primarily *The Lord of the Rings, The Lord of the Rings,* and *The Lord of the Rings.* (I was fairly selective in my reading, and once I latch onto something I like, as with any good dog, I bite down hard and don't let go. Ask my wife. The marks are still there.)

At any rate, the horror genre was something I had been hitherto unfamiliar with, and it seriously captivated me. Why do we like good scares? Why do we willingly walk into a movie theater when we know we're going to jump out of our skin? Why do we go see movies like Jaws and Alien, when everyone has told us not to go, and warned us that we would be setting our eyes on something horrifying? Perhaps because when we're perched precariously on the edge of safety, that's when we feel our senses most alive. It's a thrill ride to be scared; to not know what might be lurking around every corner; to behold something that shocks the heck out of us and imprints that trauma onto our psyche. We don't forget horror; it possesses a remarkably potent power to remain in our memory and color our trauma palette.

I went on to read other novels and stories by Stephen King, namely *Misery* – which should frighten *every* author as it still does me – *Christine, Carrie, Pet Sematary, The Long Walk,* and many more.

There is a tip of the hat to Stephen King, of course, in *Dissonance Volume I: Reality,* and those who have read it may have readily picked up on it. I think one of the marks of a good writer is being inspired by – but not copying – another writer. I have always appreciated King's twists and turns, and his incomparable ability to weave a tense narrative that is thrilling, mysterious, and full of twists.

And then you have Steven Spielberg. Namely, *Poltergeist.* Poltergeist remains one of my most favorite movies of all time, because of the sheer weight of the intangible and its hold on the waking life, and the wanderings of us sleepy humans up here. Dare we ever taunt those who have gone before, or tamper with their peace? Shouldn't they rightfully be sleeping?

Poltergeist is an immeasurably terrifying movie, one which plumbs the depths of fear as the Freeling family comes face to face with the afterlife. Tangina Barrons, the diminutive psychic star of the show utters one of the most frightening bits of dialogue ever spoken in cinematic history: *A terrible presence is in there with her. So much rage, so much betrayal. I've never sensed anything like it. I don't know what hovers over this house, but it was strong enough to punch a hole into this world and take your daughter away from you. It keeps Carol Anne very close to it and away from the spectral light. It lies to her, it tells her things only a child could understand. It has been using her to restrain the others. To her, it simply is another child. To us, it is the Beast...* *cue the shudders*

For *The Phoenix Experiment,* I wanted to tip my hat to the two Stev/phens – King and Spielberg – with my own take on interfering with the afterlife, and the horrors it can bring. The claustrophobia aboard The Origin is the exact setting I needed to do it in. You simply don't mess with what's gone before.

Spirits, phantoms, phantasms, ghosts, poltergeists, and the like… there's something inherently frightening about the intangible. How can you fight back or hide from the spirit realm, when it can pass through homes, through walls, through your very skin? Even typing that sentence gives me goosebumps.

Also, I think it's inescapable that I have no love for AI, and wanted to write something that would be a subtle referendum on the negative aspect of Artificial Intelligence. AI has laid waste to my voiceover career and the careers of many voiceover artists, as well as many of our clients. It continues to erode the natural and gorgeous process – and privilege – of creation, costing the environment, costing careers, costing relationships, costing income, costing quality of offerings, costing, costing, costing. When will we finally wake up to the cost of it? Is it neat? Sure. But a vampire is 'neat' in some respects, until you finally realize that's *your* blood that it sucked dry. Like Jeff Goldblum's character in *The Lost World* says: "Oh yeah, *oooh, ahhh,* that's how it always starts. But then later there's running, and um… screaming." I don't love AI because it's artificial. I don't love it because it's hurting careers, people, and relationships. I don't love it because it's a cheap substitute and people are too easily enamored with it, infatuated and allured by it. Just because something is neat doesn't mean that it's good. Stygius Cryptus is 'neat,' certainly.

While this novel is certainly somewhat of a departure from my normal sci-fi fare, I'm always seeking to expand my reach and try new things. *The Phoenix Experiment* is my attempt at that, and I hope it remains with you.

Special thanks to Victoria Richmond for helping me flesh out the ending narrative between Rosie and Jax!

Thank you once more to my ARC readers Jeannine Dryden, Laura Vosika and Victoria Richmond, and my audiobook reviewers Victoria Richmond and Rhonda Davis.

Special thanks to Isaac Peahi for narrating my audiobook! Try as I may, my days of being fourteen are far behind me – thank you for bringing Jax to life with honesty and drama for my audiobook listeners. Great work, Isaac!

Finally, thank you to my beautiful wife Janine for all your help in clearing up my story and helping me see, think – and write – straight. I love you. To all of you, I am so very grateful for you!

With love,

Aaron Ryan

About The Author

Award-winning and bestselling multi-genre Christian author, speaker and voice actor Aaron Ryan lives in

Washington with his wife and two sons, along with Macy the dog, Winston & Tibbles the cats, and a finch named Fry.

He is the prolific author of over 50 books, including the bestselling *Dissonance* 6-book alien invasion saga, the dystopian Christian fiction trilogies *Carbon* and *The End*, the *Talisman* epic space opera, the sci-fi thrillers F*orecast, The Slide, Blood Echoes, The Darkness Within* and *The Phoenix Experiment*, the nonfiction books *God Is Not Santa, You are my whole Earth: A Daddy's love for his Sons,* and *You're Going Straight To Helen (In A Handbasket)*, business guides, literary criticism, 6 kids picture books and more.

When he was in second grade, he was tasked with writing a creative assignment: a fictional book. And thus, *The Electric Boy* was born: a simple novella full of intrigue, fantasy, and 7-year-old wits that electrified Aaron's desire to write. From that point forward, Aaron evolved into a creative soul that desired to create.

He enjoys the arts, media, music, performing, poetry, and being a daddy. In his lifetime he has been an author, voiceover artist, wedding videographer, stage performer, musician, producer, rock/pop artist, executive assistant, service manager, paperboy, CSR, poet, tech support, worship leader, and more. The diversity of his life experiences gives him a unique approach to business, life, ministry, faith, and entertainment.

Aaron's favorite author by far is J.R.R. Tolkien, but he also enjoys Suzanne Collins, James S.A. Corey, Michael Crichton, Marie Lu, Madeleine L'Engle, John Grisham, Tom Clancy, Tim Lebbon, Christopher Golden, C.S. Lewis, Stephen King and Dave Barry. Aaron has always had a passion for storytelling.

Visit his website at https://www.authoraaronryan.com, join his exclusive Facebook group at authoraaronryangroup.com, or check out his store at authoraaronryanstore.com.

Reviews

If you liked this or any of my books, please visit the
Amazon and Goodreads pages for the specific book(s)
and leave a positive review. Once it shows up, email
the screenshot to me@authoraaronryan.com please, for
a discount on your next book purchase from me!
Thank you so much. Reviews really do help a ton, and
I'm so very grateful for you taking the time.

Connect with Aaron

Feel free to check out the following links for further information on Aaron:

Subscribe to Aaron's blog for free giveaways, news and new releases at
https://authoraaronryan.com/blog

Join the Author Aaron Ryan Facebook community at
https://facebook.com/groups/authoraaronryan

Subscribe to Aaron's YouTube channel at
https://youtube.com/@authoraaronryan

Visit Aaron's social media links to connect with him at
https://dot.cards/authoraaronryan

Follow Aaron on IMDb at
https://www.imdb.com/name/nm5976186/

Also by the Author

As Aaron Ryan:

Dissonance Volume I: Reality

Dissonance Volume II: Reckoning

Dissonance Volume III: Renegade

Dissonance Volume IV: Relentless

Dissonance Volume Zero: Revelation

Dissonance Volume Up: Rising

The Complete Dissonance Alien Invasion Saga

The End: Alpha

The End: Omicron

The End: Omega

The Complete "The End" Christian Dystopian Saga

Carbon Volume I: Programming

Carbon Volume II: Reformatting

Carbon Volume III: Rebooting

The Complete Carbon Trilogy

Forecast

The Slide

The Phoenix Experiment

Blood Echoes

The Darkness Within

Talisman: Subterfuge

Talisman: Nexus

Talisman: Halcyon

The Complete Talisman Series

The Ring of Truth

The Sword of Joy

The Book of Power

The Christian Kids Values, Identity & Affirmation Series

The Super Ordinary Heroes Series: Empathy

The Super Ordinary Heroes Series: The Invisibility Cape

The Super Ordinary Heroes Series: The Time-stopping Hug

God Is Not Santa

You are my whole Earth: A Daddy's love for his Sons

You're Going Straight To Helen (In A Handbasket)

Examining The Lord of the Rings: An independent critique by Aaron Ryan

The Superhero Anomaly

How to Successfully Self-Publish & Promote Your Independent Book: A Self-Publishing & Business Marketing Guide For The Independent Author

Reflections: A Compilation of Journals and Poetry

The Omega Room (abandoned in the early 90's)

Autobiography (no longer available)

Glimmerings – works of poetry

As his former stage name, Josh Alexander:

Voiceovers: A Super Business, A Super Life

Voiceovers: A Super Fun Pursuit

Voiceovers: A Super Responsibility

Running a Successful Voiceover Business

How do I get started in Voiceovers?

Five T's to Triumph: The Secrets to Getting Cast in Voiceovers